KISSED BY FIRE

BLOOD & MAGIC: FIREBORN - TWO

DANIELLE ANNETT

Blood & Magic

Cursed by Fire

Kissed by Fire

Burned by Fire

Branded by Fire

Consumed by Fire

Forged by Fire

—*The Book Quarry*

"This twist in Kissed by Fire was exactly what I, as a reader, needed, even though I didn't know I needed it until it happened."
—*Sapphyria's Book Blog*

"This is even better than the first one. I hope there are many more."
—*Amazon Reviewer*

Burned by Fire

"I couldn't believe how it ended either, now I'm super excited to read the next one!"
—*Shooting Stars Reviews*

"I have to say, Danielle Annett sucked me into a world of magnificent beings and creatures."
—*Amazon Reviewer*

"Ugh, these endings are killing me! I love this series. The dynamics between Naveed and [redacted] are hot, hot, hot. It just keeps getting better."
—*Amazon Reviewer*

Branded by Fire

"I have loved this series from the first book Cursed by Fire and all the characters as well. But I think that Branded by Fire is by far my favorite."
—*The Avid Reader*

"Danielle Annett's BRANDED BY FIRE is scorching hot."
—*Amazon Reviewer*

"Branded by Fire is the best one yet (and the other 3 books in the series rock!)"
—*Sapphyria's Book Blog*

Consumed by Fire

"Aria is badass"
—*Amazon Reviewer*

"Another fast paced installment of the Blood & Magic series. Aria's sass and badassery keeps me coming back for more."
—*Amazon Reviewer*

"When an author can leave you hanging and wanting more; then that is a brilliant author."
—*The Avid Reader*

Forged by Fire

"Love it. Worth the wait"
—*Amazon Reviewer*

"The conclusion to this series was everything I expected and more. Besides thinking as aria as my bff and watching her grow thru the series I've also watched this author grow. I look forward to reading her next series! She surprised me in this last book and I'm so crazy that I rarely get surprised! "
—*Amazon Reviewer*

Chapter One

I yanked at the hem of the midnight-blue dress I'd borrowed from my neighbor Melody and wondered why the hell I'd decided to wear a dress in the first place.

It was inappropriately short, below freezing outside, and I looked ridiculous.

I didn't do dresses. My wardrobe consisted of steel-toed boots, yoga pants, and t-shirts with inappropriate sayings.

So, why the hell did I let her talk me into wearing this?

I groaned. It was too late to do anything about it now.

The top sported a sweat-heart neckline that refused to stay in place. I wasn't overly busty by any means, I had boobs sure, but I didn't regularly spill out of my clothes and with my everyday clothes I could get by with a sports bra, but the stupid dress was strapless and it kept shifting leaving me feeling exposed despite the well-loved leather jacket I'd thrown over it. And don't even get me started on the bead-work encrusted top. It chafed on the underside of my arms which I was pretty sure were red and raw by now, and when the sun hit it just right, I swear the beads and their jewel like embellishments blinded me.

The whole thing was too much. Too short. Too sparkly. Too ridiculous given the weather.

Wearing anything that belonged to Melody Leis was a bad idea.

"Lesson learned," I muttered to myself and tugged on the hemline, again. Mel's fashion sense was that of a deranged punk-rock pixie. I cringed at the thought of the first dress she'd suggested I wear. It'd been pink, plaid, and pleated. PINK PLAID! How was that not criminal? I would have gone out like a boarding school reject if I'd worn her first suggestion, and you'd think after she'd pulled out that monstrosity, I would've realized her taste in clothes and mine, weren't compatible. But I'd been desperate.

Ugh! Too late to do anything about it now.

I turned away from the biting cold and faced the heavy wooden door. Its scarred surface had once been inviting. Now, the heavy door and protruding iron knocker washed a wave of dread over me.

Deeps breaths. In and out. You could do this.

I chewed on my lower lip.

Nope. I couldn't do this. Coming today had been a mistake and the dress only confirmed it. Marion wouldn't want to see me. She'd probably slam the door in my face.

And could I blame her if she did?

"Of course not." I muttered, worrying the toe of my left high heel into the snow-covered floor mat. If Marion slammed the door in my face, I couldn't and wouldn't blame her. No one wanted to see the woman responsible for their husband's death.

The peach pie in my hands was leaden between my fingers. I could turn tail and run. It wasn't too late. Did it make me a coward? Sure. Did I care …? I was undecided.

The idea of facing Marion made my chest tight and my stomach clench in an uncomfortable knot.

But I owed it to Mike to check in on her. She'd been like a

mother to me these past few years. Much as Mike had been my surrogate father. And it was my fault she was a widow now.

Taking a deep breath, I shifted the pie to one hand and lifted the other toward the heavy iron knocker. Winter air swirled around me, raising goosebumps on my bare legs.

Here goes nothing …

The door swung open.

I froze with my hand raised, caught like a deer in headlights. "Shit."

"Nice to see you too, dear." Weariness weighed down her words.

I opened my mouth then closed it. Marion Sanborn's graying hair, normally carefully styled, was pulled into a tight knot at the nape of her neck. Her wire-rimmed glasses rested on the bridge of her nose and did little to hide the dark puffy shadows that told me she'd cried recently.

I hunched my shoulders and stared listlessly down at the pie in my hands. "I …" Dammit. Words weren't coming out.

Marion reached out and tugged me into a warm embrace, the pie awkwardly held between us. "I'm glad you're here." Her vanilla-scented perfume surrounded me in a blanket of comfort. I breathed in the scent and the tight knot in my chest slowly unraveled.

She released me and gave me a quick once over, lifting a single brow when her eyes caught on my heels.

"Too much?" I wobbled for a moment before regaining my balance. The three-inch pumps hadn't been the most practical choice given the current weather or my current occupation— badass mercenary and all—But, Melody insisted I wear heels because of the dress and my closet housed two pairs of worn leather steel-toed boots, a pair of sneakers, and a single pair of flip-flops. None of which would have gone with this outfit, so I'd resigned myself to Melody's heels. I didn't have an alternative.

Though now that I was here, I wished I would have just stuck with the yoga pants and boots. I'm sure I would have been able to find at least one shirt without anything vulgar on it. I had a few solids in the back of my closet.

Marion gave me a small, but warm smile. "It's the middle of winter. Of course, it's too much. Now come inside before you freeze half to death." She turned and motioned for me to follow.

Pressing my heels into the doormat, I tried in vain to get the clumps of snow off before following.

I lingered in the entryway after I closed the door against the bitter cold.

"So … umm …" I stuttered, unable to form words. How did you say, *I'm sorry your husband is dead because of me. I wish it'd been me instead, and I wished I'd killed the bastards responsible more slowly?*

"Hush, dear. Just come have a seat."

When I didn't move, Marion bustled towards me and took the pie from my grasp. She placed it on a nearby table littered with casseroles, pies, plates of cookies, and other baked goods.

I supposed everyone else who'd come to pay their respects had thought food would help, too. I wasn't sure why I'd brought a pie, but it had seemed like the right thing to do. Now I felt like an idiot. Food didn't replace a husband.

Mike's funeral had taken place a little over three weeks ago. Looking at the array of food on the table made me realize just how loved he was. I'd gone to the funeral and watched from a distance, too afraid to face Marion at the time. Too ashamed of the role I'd played in his death. I blamed myself, and rightly so. He'd still be here if it hadn't been for me.

I'd been working a case with the Pacific Northwest Pack. Someone had murdered a seven-year-old boy to incite a war between the shifters and the local vampire Coven. I'd gotten in their way. But when they came for me, they found my boss, Mike, instead.

He'd warned me that the case was too dangerous. I should have listened. Maybe if I had, he'd still be here.

Unable to stand in the entryway any longer, I took a seat on the cream-colored sofa and folded my hands in my lap.

Marion hurried into the nearby kitchen. I heard the refrigerator open and a cupboard door close, and did my best not to fidget while I waited for her return. Anticipation ate at my nerves. Finding a stray fiber on the arm of the sofa, I pulled at the thread, trying to distract myself. For once, my pyrokinesis was silent—no sudden urges to light furniture on fire, which was a relief.

Since Mike's passing, I'd had less control over my abilities than usual. I knew a good part of it was my grief and frustration, but the lack of control was beginning to take its toll. I was glad for once it was staying dormant when I needed it to.

The pungent aroma of coffee filled the air. A few minutes later, Marion emerged from the kitchen carrying two steaming mugs. "Here, dear, drink this."

I gratefully accepted the mug of coffee she handed me, allowing the warmth to seep into my body as I brought the cup up to my mouth and took a tentative sip. Coffee had a way of soothing, and I was grateful that, like me, Marion was a coffee drinker.

I held the mug with both hands and watched Marion over the rim as she took a drink as well. She didn't look angry. Only sad. Her movements were jerky, and her lower lip trembled as she moved to set her cup aside.

If Marion started crying, I didn't know what I would do. I wasn't built to comfort others. I was harsh edges and sharp blades. Not warm and motherly. Not like Marion. My heart clenched at the thought of what she must be going through.

But I had no way to assuage her suffering.

She pulled at the edges of her cardigan, and her gaze

wandered to the left side of the room. Photographs lined the living room walls. Mike and Marion's personal hall of fame.

At Sanborn Place—the mercenary guild he'd started from the ground up—Mike had lined the walls with newspaper clippings of cases solved. The moments he was most proud of in his career.

Here, in his home, photographs lined the walls. His proudest moments as a husband. Mike and Marion had no children, but they'd traveled all over the country, and they proudly displayed those memories for guests to see—A photograph of the two of them at the Santa Cruz beach boardwalk. Another in San Antonio, Texas in front of The Alamo.

My gaze landed on their wedding portrait. It hung as the focal point of the room, above the fireplace mantel. They must have been little more than teenagers. Both so young and so in love.

When I returned my attention to Marion, the corners of her mouth lifted into a small smile, though the sadness remained in her eyes.

"We had twenty great years together," she told me.

Moisture pooled in the corners of my eyes and I blinked them away. "I'm so, so sorry." God, wasn't that the truth. Mike and Marion had taken me in when I had no one else. And how had I repaid them? They had deserved better from me.

I rubbed a fisted hand over my chest.

"For what? You didn't take him from me."

I couldn't look up. I fought the emotions threatening to emerge and set my coffee mug aside on the nearby end table.

"It was my fault." I hung my head. "They came for me and killed him instead. He wouldn't have even been there had I not asked him to look into someone for me." The "someone" being Viola Reynolds. The mother I'd long believed dead.

She'd fooled me. Abandoned me at the age of seventeen and

left me alone to fend for myself, believing both she and my father died gruesome deaths. My Papa had. But all this time, she'd been alive and well, living under an alias as the leader of the Human Alliance Corporation.

I almost laughed at the irony. I'd found my long-lost mother only to lose my beloved surrogate father.

Marion reached out and clasped my hand in hers. "We knew the dangers of his line of work. Don't carry that guilt with you. It's not your burden. It'll only weigh you down."

I appreciated her words. But I didn't agree with them. Mike's death would follow me no matter where I went. He'd meant too much to me for it not to.

A tear slipped free and slid down my cheek. I hastily wiped it away with the back of my hand.

"Now that you're here, there are some things I'd like to discuss with you."

I nodded, still not bothering to look up as Marion released my hand.

Papers ruffled close by. I sniffed and took a hard swallow, the lump in my throat refusing to go down.

"Mike left Sanborn Place to you," she said without any preamble. "He'd prepared his will last year and named you the beneficiary of both his business and the building in the event of his death."

A flash of surprise coursed through me, and I winced at the mention of the building. Mike died in my arms, and when his attackers returned for me, I'd killed them in a blaze of fury that'd left the office in ruins. I wasn't sure how much of the building survived.

"Why would he leave Sanborn Place to me?" Her words sank in, and the reality of it hit me full force. "Why me? Why not Nico or Taylor?" They were the veteran mercs. The ones with a hell of a lot more experience. I had no idea how to run a business. I was twenty-three. I didn't go to college. Everything I knew was what I learned along the way.

Marion's eyes softened as she handed me a few sheets of paper. My hands shook as I read over each page line by line. Mike named me his sole beneficiary for the business. He'd added my name to the deed on Sanborn Place. It was mine free and clear. Why would he do that?

"Nico and Taylor are great mercenaries. But they were only ever employees. You know he always thought of you as a daughter. The daughter we were never able to have." Marion's words were full of emotions I couldn't quite grasp.

This couldn't be real.

She reached forward and clasped my hand between both of hers. "Aria, you're family. You'll always be welcome here. Hopefully, by taking over Sanborn Place, you'll finally realize you're one of ours." Her hands were warm, her grasp frail yet firm.

I stared into her golden-brown eyes, my heart blooming inside my chest. Her eyes were so much like my own. A physical feature that connected me to the family I hadn't been born into, but that accepted me anyway.

Could she really mean it?

"This isn't right." Sanborn Place was Mike's life. He'd started the company from nothing. I'd been a merc for only a handful of years. I knew I hadn't earned my stripes. "I don't deserve it. You should keep it. Hell, you should sell it. I know the money could help you live comfortably. You deserve that."

Decision made, I implored her with my eyes. I couldn't keep something this important. No matter how badly I wanted to. I could find work at another guild. I had savings. I'd be fine. "Sell it. If it's in my name already, I'll sign it over to you. It's yours."

Marion gently touched my cheek, her eyes soft.

"It's yours. Sanborn Place took my husband from me. I want no part of it." Her tone broached no argument. "His client files are in this box." She indicated a large cardboard file box beside the sofa. "He kept copies of everything at home so you won't have to worry about those lost in the fire."

I flinched. I wanted to apologize for the fire. For taking away his body and leaving her nothing but ash to bury. But I couldn't. I didn't trust myself not to fall apart.

When Mike was killed, it was like someone ripped my heart from my chest. Nightmares plagued me. I lost my appetite. I could feel myself wasting away, but none of it mattered. Not when—

Marion's voice interrupted my thoughts. "I didn't want you facing it the way it was, so I hired a crew to repair the damage. They told me they should complete renovations within the next two weeks." Marion reached into the pocket of her sweater and retrieved a business card, handing it to me. "You're welcome to stop by the site anytime, and the owner assured me you can call anytime if you have questions or want to make any changes."

Diamond Rock Construction was written across the black surface in simple but sleek embossed lettering. I rubbed a finger over the smooth soft matte finish. The only other information on the card was a phone number, no personal name to go with it.

"Sanborn Place is yours. Don't feel like you can't make changes."

I stayed for another hour, doing my best to remain upbeat. Marion fixed the two of us lunch from the variety of casseroles friends and relatives had brought over. I pushed the food around my plate, hoping it looked like I was actually eating, but I was pretty sure Marion caught on when she continued to offer me alternatives. Pie. Rice Pudding. Kale salad. It all looked great, but my stomach revolted at the idea of being filled with any of it.

She'd barely touched her own food. The grief weighing on her was all too visible, as though it were a physical thing. I wished I knew what to say, how to help.

As I prepared to leave, I promised Marion I'd stay in touch

and visit often. I wasn't sure if it was a promise I could keep. My guilt over Mike's death ate at me every minute of every day. Part of me thought it'd be easier if Marion decided she didn't want to see me again.

It was a selfish thought.

Chapter Two

I drove straight to Sanborn Place, curious about what progress they had made in the month since Mike's death. With winter in full swing, most of downtown Spokane's sidewalks were empty. A small group of homeless people clustered beneath the freeway around fires burning inside metal garbage cans for warmth.

My tires slid on the wet pavement as I took the exit that would lead me to Sanborn Place. The streets were icing up, and when I took a corner faster than I should have, I had to jerk on the wheel to keep from spinning out of control.

Adrenaline spiked, and small flames broke out along my skin. I muttered a curse and forced my breathing to even out before drawing the flames back inside me.

Righting my Civic, I pulled into the underground parking garage, parked, and headed up the staircase leading to the main doors. The garage housed an elevator that would quickly take me to the first-floor office, but elevators and I weren't on good terms.

Walking inside through the exterior doors, the acidic smell of paint and primer hit me in the face. Several men dressed in worn jeans and long-sleeved Carhartt T-shirts, with worn leather tool belts fastened around their waists, milled about painting, patching holes in the drywall, and tearing out burnt remnants of carpet.

No one seemed to pay me any mind. I got a few nods as I walked in, but no one seemed concerned I was here.

The smell of paint made my nose sting as I walked through the office. But the smell of burnt flesh was unmistakable beneath it—the thick, cloying scent of decay mixed with the acrid smell of charred meat.

I grimaced and covered my mouth as I fought to keep what little I'd eaten at Marion's down. "You're just imagining it," I muttered to myself. I had to be. The construction workers looked unbothered by the smell. It had to be me. Right?

I took a deep breath through my mouth.

You can never really get the smell of burning flesh out of your nose entirely, Mike had once said.

And I had to agree.

I stopped short when I came to the part of the office where the attack had taken place. The blood-stained carpet was gone, but in my mind, I could still see Mike's prone form lying beside his desk as his blood pooled all around him.

I swallowed the lump in my throat and forced my feet to carry me forward.

Memories that had since become my nightmares struck. A flash just before the room ignited. The sizzle of vampire flesh. The ash of the Vampire's body falling like grey snow from a darkened sky to land on my cheeks.

I lifted my hand to my face and shook the memory away.

The burn marks on the walls left streaks of black and brown in the grisly outline of a body. I'd done that. I'd caused ruin in a place I thought of as a second home.

The night Mike died, my powers had exploded in a wave of destruction I hadn't realized I was capable of. It'd both terrified and exhilarated me to feel the surge of adrenaline and the rush of fire through my veins. It was like being on a drug. Addicting. All-consuming.

It'd been weightless. Lost in my fury until reality came crashing down to rock bottom. Leaving me with nothing but my grief.

I was glad the people responsible had died a painful death at my hands—though their deaths had been too quick. My rage had bubbled beneath the surface of my skin, unquenched despite the vampire's only remains being the ashes their bodies left behind. But it wasn't enough. I was still angry at everyone, at fate, at myself, at how unfair it all was, and even worse, I was bitter.

It left a sour taste in my mouth and a gaping hole in my chest.

I'd never been more grateful for my pyrokinetic abilities than when I'd pinned one of the vampires who'd attacked Mike to the wall with my blades and funneled my fire into him. I'd watched him burn from the inside out. His flesh had glowed molten red, reminiscent of lava before a loud pop. His body had exploded in a cascade of smoldering ash. But I'd wanted more. I wished I could bring him back just to kill him again and again.

Before this, I'd always tried to hide my pyrokinetic abilities. I'd been warned from a young age to keep them secret. Factions of paranormals were always at odds. I never wanted to be the weapon used to win a war or to become some lab rat for the humans.

But now all bets were off, and all of my cards were on the table. The Coven knew what I could do. So did the Pack. And Inarus—I shook my head. He knew, and he was probably the most dangerous. But I refused to hide anymore. If they wanted a piece of me, they could come and try to get it. I was itching for a fight.

Fire bubbled beneath the surface of my skin. Almost as though my blood constantly simmered, the heat in my body no longer lying dormant. No longer willing to remain contained.

It scared the shit out of me, especially when I thought about just how much power I had. How much devastation I could bring, and how little control I really had over all of it.

But I couldn't let fear overwhelm me. So, I did the next best thing.

I funneled it into my anger. Was it healthy? Probably not. Did I care? Not really. We all dealt with grief in our own way. This was mine.

A man crouched on the floor placing baseboard trim and he looked strangely familiar. He lifted his head as I neared and gave me a brief nod in a way of greeting.

"Hi," I stopped beside him and gave him a weak wave.

He brushed his hands off on his jeans and stood to face me. Rich tan skin like my own, a friendly smile, and chocolate-colored eyes met my gaze.

"Do I know you?" I cocked my head to the side and gave him another once over.

"Yes, and no. I'm Christian, Christian Kennedy. I'm the general contractor here on site. We haven't formally met, but you might remember me from your stay with the Pack. We've passed one another in the halls at the Compound a time or two."

Wait. The halls at the Compound? He was a shifter? I looked beyond his casual, working-man facade, and I saw the predator beneath. The glint in his chocolate-colored eyes, the slight reflective quality common to shifters. It wasn't obvious, but it was there, hiding just below the surface.

"Is Diamond Rock Construction Pack owned?" I folded my arms across my chest as irritation unfurled inside me. How was the Pack finagling its way into every crevice of my life? I knew the Pack had several business ventures, but hadn't known they owned a construction company.

Having the Pack involved in my place of work unsettled me. I already owed Declan for giving me a safe place to stay. I couldn't afford to owe him any more favors. Especially since they were likely to be ones I couldn't or wouldn't deliver on.

"It is," a familiar voice said from behind me.

My shoulders stiffened, and the hairs on the back of my neck stood on end. *Sonovabitch.*

I turned to see Declan Valkenaar prowl my way. He commanded the room, and everyone he passed acknowledged his presence with deference.

Just my luck. The Alpha was here.

"I'll take it from here, Christian."

Christian nodded and bent back down to his work.

"What are you doing here?" I didn't bother to tone down the harshness of my question.

Declan was ruthless, and I knew he had an ulterior motive when it came to me even if I didn't know what he wanted yet. He'd maintained control of the Pacific Northwest Pack for the last nine years. Unchallenged. Something that was virtually unheard of among shapeshifter packs.

Declan wanted something. People like him always did, and I wasn't naïve enough to think he was being helpful because he was a nice guy. I knew he wanted to use me and my pyrokinetic abilities to his advantage. The fact that he'd yet to ask for anything didn't have me fooled. The request would come eventually. I had no doubt.

A war was brewing between the Pack and the local vampire Coven. The shaky truce between the two factions was a truce in name alone. Neither side had any intentions of playing nice. Declan wouldn't attack unprovoked, but he would make sure he was ready and in position to win should the Coven strike out against his people.

Rogue vampires killed Mike. It made me want to hate them all. But I couldn't hold the entire Coven responsible for something they'd had no control over. Declan might think I was a perfectly made weapon for fighting vampires, but I wasn't going to be his weapon. The Pack would not own me. And when push came to shove, I was Switzerland. He'd have to fight his own battles.

Declan quirked a blond brow in amusement, his nostrils flaring as he undoubtedly took in my scent.

Wonderful. Just what I wanted—to amuse him.

"I'm checking up on the job. Is that a problem?" His voice was a deep timbre that had every one of my senses on high alert. Because yes, it was a problem.

I didn't want him in my business. But I didn't have a tactful way to say that. If the construction company was owned by the Pack, he had every right to come and check on their progress. It shouldn't have bothered me, but it did.

The last month had been grating on my nerves. Someone was always watching me. And for being the Alpha of one of the biggest known packs in the United States, Declan was oddly available. Always close by. Always aware of my every move. And always telling me what I should or shouldn't do to stay safe. He wasn't my keeper, and I didn't need a babysitter.

I swear the man had eyes in the back of his head and ears in every room.

"Nope. No problem. But don't you have more important things to do?" I gritted my teeth and forced out a smile.

He shook his head, and a smile tugged at the corner of his mouth, "I make time for all of my people."

Right. I bet he did. The thing was, I wasn't one of his people.

He eyed me up and down, his emerald gaze lingering on the exposed skin of my legs before being drawn down to my high heels and back up again.

What? Never seen a girl in a dress and heels before?

I bit the inside of my cheek to keep from saying anything stupid, but I needed to say something, anything, and then get the hell out of here. I went for casual, "Good to know. I was just passing through, so I'll see you around." I waved, but as I moved to leave, he reached out and grasped my forearm. I'd left my jacket in the car, and his calloused palm against my bare skin sent a flood of sensation through me.

His grip was firm as he held me immobile.

I resisted the urge to jerk free of his grasp. Instead, smiling wide with all the false sincerity I could muster, I lifted a single brow and stared him square in the eyes.

His tiger met my gaze, and his eyes turned molten.

I still didn't look away. Seconds passed, and the tension grew thick between us. I could feel the gazes of the men around us as the tension thickened. But, locked in my self-induced battle, I couldn't look away.

A growl rumbled behind me, and I blinked.

Dammit.

The tension instantly dissipated, and Declan spoke as though nothing had just happened.

"Aren't you interested in our progress?" Declan's casual tone did nothing to hide his intense Alpha presence. "I can show you some of the improvements we've made."

Those piercing emerald green eyes of his were hard as granite. I wasn't a shifter, but now, even I wanted to turn my gaze away in submission. It was a struggle, but I kept my eyes locked on his again. He might win in a staring contest, but I knew it still annoyed the hell out of him when I held his gaze.

And hell yes, I was petty enough to enjoy his irritation.

"That's okay. I'll wait until everything is finished." Without another word, I pulled my arm free from his grasp and made my way out the main doors.

Outside, I released a breath of relief and shook my head to clear my thoughts. I should move back to my apartment. Being in such close proximity to Declan on a reoccurring basis was getting to me. If I didn't leave soon, I would punch him in the teeth. And then I'd be the one inciting a war with the Pack.

It had started to snow, just a light sprinkling that added to the thin layer already coating the pavement. I folded my arms across my chest and hunched my shoulders against the wind. *Why had I left my jacket in the car?*

I'd just turned to head toward the stairs that would lead me to my car when the late afternoon quiet shattered.

"Run!" A man barreled towards me, his open overcoat flapping around his knees. "Run!" Outright panic filled his manic expression as he flew past me.

I jumped back to avoid being crashed into and nearly fell, my back scraping the brick wall of Sanborn Place.

Ow! That hurt.

With wide eyes, I watched the guy fly down the sidewalk and around the corner before I turned to look the way he'd just come.

I froze, flattening my body against the cold brick. *You have got to be kidding me!*

A man approached, slowly at first, the flurries of snow making it difficult to see him clearly. But there was something predatory about his determined gait.

My blood ran cold for the first time in weeks, and the hairs on my neck rose on end. Everything in me screamed that I needed to run just as the man had instructed.

Breath lodged in my throat, I pushed myself away from the building just as two women exited a small shop across the street, their arms full with their purchases.

"Go back inside!" I yelled, waving my arms frantically.

The women looked at me like I was crazy.

I swore and tried again. "Go. Get back! It's not safe."

Instinct told me to leave them behind. But I couldn't. They were clearly human. Two very normal, very human women who wouldn't stand a chance against what was heading our way.

"Vampire!" I yelled.

Their gazes jerked toward me and then to the oncoming man. Shaking their heads and laughing as though I were delusional, they continued on their way, heading down the sidewalk at too slow of a pace. They still didn't see it.

Fooled by the media and vampire propaganda, humans were under the impression that vampires came out only at night.

That wasn't true.

Newly-made vamps did just fine in the daylight for short periods of time. Not that you'd see them wandering around much. Baby vamp equaled fragile vamp so while sunlight in thirty to sixty-minute spurts wouldn't kill them, being slaughtered by a shifter or mage would and without their maker around, they were free game.

I couldn't think of a situation where a vampire would take the time to turn a human only to leave them on their own, all but defenseless against the rest of the paranormal population. Vampires tended to be loners sure, but newly-made vampires needed care. They needed someone to show them how to feed. How to manage their heightened senses.

They also needed time to recover. The change wasn't a slow or easy process. It required an individual to be drained almost entirely of blood. Brought to the edge of death, a vampire would then feed them their own blood to replenish what they had taken. The process had to be repeated a minimum of three times —sometimes more if the vampire wasn't old and powerful enough to stop at three—before the magic in a vampire's blood took effect and granted the once human immortality.

Most couldn't hold on to the thin thread of life after being drained long enough to feed. And often the vampire performing the transition couldn't fight back their own bloodlust and took things one step too far.

The grueling process was why most humans didn't survive the transition.

This one had. So where was his maker?

This afternoon's overcast skies and sprinkling of snow were perfect conditions for any baby vamp to explore the city with their maker close by. There was little to no risk of direct sun exposure. Being careful, a vampire could last several hours outside during days like today. So, with that in mind, why was this baby vamp left alone?

I jerked forward into the street and scanned the area for any other passersby. Maybe his maker was somewhere lurking in the shadows, and I just hadn't seen him. Traffic in the area was light at this time of day. Most unwilling to brave the winter cold. Thank God for small blessings.

I saw no signs of any other vampire in the vicinity.

This wasn't good. I considered stepping back inside. Sanborn Place was a strong building easily capable of keeping out one baby vamp but no… I pursed my lips together. I couldn't just leave him out on the loose where he could happen across a defenseless human. I'd find out who'd made him, and I'd contain or kill him if it came to that.

If he latched on to a human, it would be a bloodbath.

Facing the vampire now, I saw the moment he locked his eyes on me, the red glow evident even from the twenty-foot distance. His mouth curved into a freakish smile as his canines extended over his lower lip, his fingers curling as though he had claws.

A chilling realization thrummed through me. He was a predator. And I was prey. I was reconsidering the whole baby vamp equals fragile vamp notion.

The women finally took notice. Horror washed over their faces. *About time.* They ran, dropping their purchases in their haste.

I waited for the bloodsucker to go after them. The easy prey. Predators went after the first thing that caught their attention and always aimed for the easy kill. Two human women running for their lives—arms flailing, packages falling—should have nabbed his attention immediately. But he didn't even look their way. His focus stayed on me.

Alrighty then. It looked like today was my lucky day.

My fire called to me. It begged me to bring it forth, whispering to me to destroy my foe in one quick strike. Tempting. But something wasn't right about the situation. A newly made vampire walking the streets of downtown Spokane as if he were on a leisurely stroll?

The change had to have been recent. Blood soaked his light blue shirt, leaving a large stain on his chest and the left side of his body. If I had to guess, he'd been changed less than twenty-four hours ago. His skin hadn't turned the pale milky white associated with the undead yet. It could take up to a week before a changed human gained the near-perfect complexion of a vampire. And up to a month before they had complete control over their heightened senses and bloodlust.

But before I could dwell on that tidbit of information, he struck.

In a split second, his once jerky movements morphed into a flash of speed as he launched himself at me. His movements were little more than a blur.

I twisted out of the way but was too slow. He grabbed me by the back of the neck and flung me across the road like a rag doll.

Nope. Not weak. Not fragile. Damn.

I sailed through the air, trying to twist myself into a position that would have me landing on my feet.

Instead, I collided with a parking meter. The nearly frozen metal split my cheek and knocked the air from my lungs.

Goddammit. I wiped the trail of blood that dripped down my face with the back of my hand and exhaled a vicious curse. "You're going to pay for that." I pulled my twin daggers from the thigh sheath beneath my dress and jumped to my feet. My dress rode up, but I couldn't have cared less at the moment. I was sure the vamp didn't care either.

A flash of leg wasn't what his red filled gaze was glued too. No. The blood that trickled down my cheek had his nostrils flaring, and vicious hunger stamped across his face.

My ribs ached with my movements, but I blocked out the pain. "You can get a Band-Aid later," I told myself.

He charged again. I dug my heels into the icy pavement, allowing the vampire to get close, his hands brushing my shoulders, and his fangs fully extended as he lunged for my neck.

I forced my body to relax. Almost there.

His hot breath brushed my skin just before I sank my first blade into the soft flesh of his stomach. It slid in with sickening ease, and he twitched like he'd been zapped by lightning.

I plunged my second blade into his chest, barely missing his heart. On purpose, of course. I wanted to slow him down. Not kill him.

Vampires could be killed a number of ways. Losing their heads, losing their hearts, and being burned alive were the main ones. Their flesh was highly flammable. One lick of fire and poof, they'd go up like the fourth of July.

A dagger to the heart under normal circumstances would only paralyze, not kill. But my daggers were imbued with silver—the only metal to adversely affect both vampires and shifters—and this vamp was young. I wasn't certain that a stab to the heart wouldn't kill him, and I wasn't willing to risk it.

With my daggers still embedded in his chest and stomach, he squeezed my shoulder, the pain explosive. I heard a distinct pop before my left arm went limp.

Fuck!

My brain took a backseat as adrenaline flowed through my muscles. I kicked out with my left foot, the heel of my pump sinking into his calf.

His leg buckled, allowing me to pull away. I lost my heel in the process, and cold slush squished beneath my toes. I ignored the unpleasant feeling and ripped one of my blades free, forced to leave the other in his chest.

My left arm hung loosely at my side, and I had to refrain from clamping it close to my body. I needed my free hand to fight, but each sway of my injured arm sent a jolt of pain down my spine.

Nausea threatened to consume me. I gritted my teeth. Vomiting in the middle of a fight was so not going to happen.

Just keep it together, Ari! You can do this.

I raised my right hand and tightened my grip on my dagger. Dark red blood dripped from its tip.

The vampire's eyes glowed an even deeper red, fangs descending farther to cover his bottom lip.

You might as well put those back, mister. You won't be making a meal out of me.

Hot blood surged through my veins. I hastily kicked off my remaining heel, ignoring the discomfort of the snow and gravel beneath my feet. I needed to move faster.

When he lunged again, I threw myself to the left, lifting my right hand to slash his throat in a swift upward arc.

A gurgling sound emanated from his throat, but he didn't bother to clutch the wound. His body was already working to knit the skin back together. Blood seeped through his neck and from the corners of his mouth, but if I'd hurt him, I couldn't tell.

Damn vampire.

My fire called insistently, demanding to take charge. I shoved it down with everything I had, which wasn't a lot at this point.

I was determined to find out who had turned him, and why he'd been set loose. I needed him alive for that.

Well, as alive as an undead could be.

I moved to deliver another deep stab to his stomach. But just as I moved to strike, a thunderous growl echoed through the streets.

Like an idiot, I turned at the sound of another predator making itself known.

The moment of distraction cost me, and I could barely block my neck with my free hand in time. The vampire sank his teeth into my forearm. An angry scream ripped free from my throat, and blinding pain raced up my arm.

The growl turned into an ear-splitting roar.

Fucking great. Declan Valkenaar has arrived. Even my sarcasm couldn't be squelched by the pain.

I watched narrow-eyed as Declan charged forward. My body wanted to run away from the savage man barreling towards me, but vampire fangs buried in my flesh had me locked in place as Declan tackled the baby vampire from behind.

He brought him to the ground with a sickening crunch of bone that echoed loud in my ears.

I'd tried to get out of his way at the last second, but the stupid vamp refused to let go. I wound up in a heap beside them, my arm now missing a chunk of flesh as blood flowed freely from the wound to stain the snow-covered ground.

Declan's motions were a blur in my peripheral vision as claws ripped through his fingertips to sink into the vampire's neck.

I staggered back on hands and knees as Declan ripped into the vampire, throwing hunks of flesh behind him as he tore through muscle in search of bone.

I tried to staunch the bleeding in my right arm with my left hand, but couldn't get my arm to cooperate.

"Screw it." I needed to stop this. He couldn't kill the vampire. Not yet.

Pulling myself to my feet, I tried to shuffle forward when Declan's claws finally scraped bone. The sound was like nails on a chalkboard.

"Don't—" I shouted, but his beast was in control.

Declan encircled the vampire's neck with both hands buried deep in his flesh and, in one quick movement, snapped it. He pulled a length of vertebrae free and threw it to the pavement beside him.

I cringed.

The vampire twitched once before the body sank deeper into

the pavement. Desiccation never took long when the undead experienced their final death.

Declan rose from the crumpled body, his chest heaving with battle fury. His chest and arms were bathed in blood, and he looked like a Viking warrior ready for round two.

The corners of his lips lifted in a silent snarl.

He delivered one hard kick to the vampire's head and grunted in satisfaction when it rolled several feet away.

He wouldn't be getting up after that.

As though a switch had been flipped, I snapped out of my daze. Fury and frustration rose to the surface. "What the hell did you just do?" I yelled at him.

Don't light the Alpha on fire. Don't light the Alpha on fire. I repeated the mantra over and over in my head. It would not bode well for me to attack him right now. No matter how much he deserved it.

Declan looked taken aback for a moment. The gold faded from his eyes, leaving twin jewels of emerald. "I saved your life."

Urgh. Moron! "No, you didn't. You didn't even think about what you were doing." My temperature rose, and I had to take a calming breath to contain myself.

It didn't help.

"Why would I think about it? He had his fangs buried in your arm. I'd expect a little gratitude here."

I stormed past him and crouched beside the vampire. Tearing my dagger from his chest, I wiped the blade on the hem of my dress and sheathed it. The dress was already ruined. A little more blood couldn't hurt it.

I needed something else to focus on aside from Declan's stupidity, or I was going to lose what little control I had. I skimmed my hands over the cold and sunken body, checking the pockets of his shirt and pants, hoping to find something that might provide me with some sort of clue.

I gagged once, but could otherwise keep it together. The

headless corpse was shriveling as his immortality leaked from his body, and I tried to ignore the beef jerky texture of his skin when my hand brushed over it.

The clouds parted and rays of sunlight pierced the ground. The vamp would be ash soon.

"What are you doing?" Declan's tone was annoyed.

Join the club, buddy. I was pretty damn annoyed myself. "I'm looking for information." I bit out. I didn't bother looking up. "It would have been much easier to just question the vampire, but no, you had to go and rip out his neck and be all 'I am tiger, hear me roar.'" I threw my hands in the air in frustration. "You didn't have to sever his vertebrae entirely. You could have easily disabled him by snapping his neck but leaving it intact."

He snarled beside me. "I saved your life."

"No. You interfered. I'm a pyrokinetic. Don't you think if I'd wanted him dead, I'd have lit his ass on fire? I didn't want him dead. I wanted him disabled."

Declan snorted. "Yeah, you were doing a great job."

I whirled on him and speared a finger into his chest. "I was doing just fine until you barged in all hot-headed and killed him." I swore under my breath and bent back down to continue searching the vampire's coat pockets.

Bingo. I pulled out a piece of paper, folded into a thick square.

Standing up, I struggled to unfold it single-handed, my left arm still hanging limp at my side.

"Let me." Declan snatched the square from my hand and unfolded it. His eyes grew dangerously dark as he stared at whatever the paper revealed.

"Give me that." I leaned toward him and snatched the paper from his hands.

He snarled, but didn't take it back.

I held out a photograph of me. I'd been walking across the

street near my apartment complex. The outfit I'd been wearing had been one I'd worn just last week.

Shit.

Who'd given this vampire a photograph of me, and why?

"Well, I hope you're happy," I said. "Now we'll never know why he had my picture in his pocket, will we?"

A deep growl reverberated through Declan's chest.

I bit my cheek and glared at him, refusing to back down. "Next time, maybe use your head and ask questions first and kill the bad guy later. I huffed out a breath and turned away, walking towards the stairs that led to the parking garage at Sanborn Place.

I was not going to stand there while he got all growly at me.

Declan kept pace beside me, a stern expression on his face. "Where are you going?" he demanded.

"None of your business." Okay, that was childish, but could he go away now?

"You're hurt. Your injuries need to be checked out."

I snorted. Way to point out the obvious, but I could take care of myself. What I really needed was to get away from him before I punched him in the face.

I smiled and briefly closed my eyes to visualize my fist connecting with his smug face. Satisfaction thrummed through me.

"Aria—"

"It's a scratch. I'm fine." I didn't need him fussing over me.

His hand on my shoulder stopped me. "Aria, I'm not just talking about the bite. You dislocated your shoulder. You need to have it reduced."

"I'll take care of it," I ground out.

Declan's grip tightened.

Ow!

I stared into his eyes for a beat before conceding. Fine, if he wanted to be a control freak, we'd do this here and now. At least it would save me the trouble of driving home one-handed. It was a bitch with a stick shift, but I'd managed it before.

Adjusting his grip, he placed one hand on my left shoulder, the other on my bicep. His eyes met mine once more, and he waited.

I said nothing, just stared into the fathomless pools of emerald green, watching the flecks of gold dance within his irises.

Lost in the motion, I felt my body sway as though tempted to dance to the silent rhythm.

Without warning, he jerked my arm up. The joint popped back into place, and a pained cry escaped my lips.

He released his hold and stepped back.

I cradled my elbow, hugging my arm close as I rode through the sharp wave of pain. The adrenaline that had fueled my body was long gone, and I felt every bit of the aching hurt now.

A full minute passed before I could think clearly. I took several deep breaths, like I'd practiced in meditation, and pushed the pain to the furthest recesses of my mind. "Thank you, Mr. Valkenaar." I moved to leave when he stopped me once more. "Now what?" I was exhausted, and my entire body throbbed with pain. I just wanted to go home.

Declan lifted a hand, claws extending from his nail beds. With a quick motion he pulled the hem of his T-shirt away from his body, then ripped a thick strip free with his claws. He carefully lifted my bleeding arm towards him, wound the fabric tightly around it, and tied a quick knot to keep the bandage secure. "There."

I scowled down at the makeshift bandage. What was he playing at here? Declan didn't do nice. He was dominant. An Alpha-asshole through and through.

He gave me a quick once over. "Any other injuries I'm missing?"

I shook my head. "I'm good. Thanks."

"Don't mention it."

We stared at one another, the tension thick between us but, surprisingly, not uncomfortable.

A car zipped down the road in our direction, forcing me to break eye contact and get out of the street.

I turned away and retrieved my heels from the pavement, and headed back to the garage, seeking the comfort of my vehicle. I didn't look back, and Declan didn't follow.

Chapter Three

Thirty minutes later, the heavy iron-gate leading to the Pack Compound greeted me. The Pack crest stood out in the gate's center like a beacon, drawing my attention. The emblem was round. Thick evergreens filled the lower half of the crest, with high-peaked mountains behind them and to the right.

In the top left corner was a crescent moon and in the space where the top and bottom of the moon formed its points was a paw print. The one part that gave me pause was the very bottom. At first, you might think it was a river bleeding through the trees, but on closer inspection, you realized it was a trail of blood spilling over the circle that surrounded the crest.

The Pack would always defend what was theirs.

Nestled on one hundred and seven acres of timberland in northeastern Washington, the Compound stood ten stories high, each level roughly seventy-four thousand square feet.

It reminded me of Costco. If you stacked ten of them one on top of one another.

It was home to nearly eight hundred shifters—though as a whole, the Pacific Northwest Pack counted closer in the thousands—it was the largest Pack in North America and spread across Washington, Oregon, Idaho, and parts of Montana with their main fortress in Spokane, Washington.

The Pack consisted of six Clans. Each led by a single—or joint, if mated—Clan Alpha, and all of them served under Declan Valkenaar, the Pack Alpha.

The Pacific Northwest Pack was made up of Clans Wolf, Cat, Feloidea, Muridae, Canidae, and Big, which encompassed, well, anything really big. Bears, a handful of water buffalos, and, if memory served, a rhinoceros shifter or two.

It used to be Clan Bear, but I guess they decided to diversify and couldn't come up with a better Clan name. Because let's be honest, Clan Big was pretty lame.

Not that it made any difference to me.

Brock stood by the front gate—the Pack's resident head of security. He was a lion shifter in his mid-twenties who'd yet to fill out entirely. His long limbs, boyish features, and ever-present smile clashed hard with what you'd think a head of security looked like. But Brock used that to his advantage.

He liked when he was underestimated.

I slowed my Honda Civic to a stop at the entrance and offered him a mock salute, to which he just rolled his cognac-colored eyes.

"I heard you got yourself into some trouble this afternoon."

Of course he did.

I drummed my fingers along my steering wheel. "Nothing I couldn't handle," I said and tried to keep the annoyance I was feeling out of my voice. "You going to let me in?"

Brock paused as if he had to think about it. "You gonna dress up like that more often?"

I snorted. "Hard no. It does a shit job hiding the blood."

He nodded his head. "Probably a good idea. Don't need to give anyone any ideas." He waggled his eyebrows, and I couldn't contain my laugh.

"Right because I'm such a hot commodity."

He waggled his eyebrows. "You never know?"

I laughed so hard my stomach cramped. "I'm a hazard to myself and others. Trust me, this—" I swept a hand over my dress, "does nothing for anyone."

Brock gave me another once over, his gaze lingering on my chest before sweeping up to my face.

"Maybe. Maybe not."

Heat crept up my face. "Right. Well, you gonna let me in or what?"

He smiled and waved me forward. "Be sure to ask James what he thinks of the dress when you see him."

I flipped him the bird and pulled through the gates. With any luck, James wouldn't see the dress before I had a chance to burn it.

I parked to the left of the main entrance and didn't bother to lock the doors as I got out and headed for the main doors. What would be the point? I was in what was probably the most secure building in all of Washington.

I navigated the intricate hallways of the enormous Compound, heels in hand and blood still dripping down my forearm. I was grateful that no one stopped me along my way. My first order of business was to grab some coffee from the kitchen. I needed caffeine, or I would crash, hard.

Injuries meant my body had to kick it into high gear to speed up the healing process. I burned through calories the way a gas-guzzling truck burned through fuel. I should eat but—

My stomach grumbled and tightened, creating a hollow ache low in my belly. I found a pile of muffins on the counter and snagged two before heading to my room. With any luck, I'd be able to keep one or both down.

I took an enormous bite of the first one. Blueberry and lemon burst along my taste buds, but it didn't give me the same sense of satisfaction it should have, but I forced myself to take a second bite. Then a third. Right now I needed the fuel, so I'd push myself to eat for that reason alone.

Once inside the confines of my bedroom, I tossed the heels on the floor, threw my leather jacket on the bed, and settled into the lone lounge chair to eat my muffins. I curled my toes into the carpet, the plush material scrunching beneath my bare feet.

So much better than slush between your toes.

Not five minutes passed when there was a knock at the door. *Crap.* "One minute."

I stripped out of my dress, threw it on the floor, and slipped into a pair of black yoga pants and a cotton T-shirt, wincing as I slid my arms in. This one said, *Feeling IDGAF-ish Today.* Maybe I'd make it my motto for the day. Or hell, the week.

I'd scarfed down one of the muffins, so with the other in hand, I answered the door to find a man holding a tray piled high with food.

I eyed him warily. "Can I help you?"

Dressed casually in jeans, a white tee, and a pair of Converse sneakers, the man outside my door was familiar, but I couldn't remember his name. He ran his hand through his short blonde hair, eyes downcast.

Was he a submissive?

I waited in the doorway and took another bite of my muffin.

Seconds ticked by before he straightened his spine and offered me a dazzling smile. He was good-looking. Short blond hair, hazel eyes, a square jaw, and perfectly straight white teeth. He had the typical corded muscles like most shifters, but I was a sucker for good teeth.

"I… umm… I brought this for you." He shoved the tray into my hands, and I struggled to juggle it and my muffin. I hissed when the tray brushed again my injured forearm. "You know, in case you were hungry." He ran his free hand through his blond hair again, and I stared down at the tray.

He'd really loaded the thing down with meat. There was a ham steak, scrambled eggs, bacon, and sausage. More than any normal person could possibly eat in one sitting. A small bowl of sliced strawberries and a small glass of orange juice perched on the side.

I eyed him suspiciously for a moment. Good looks didn't mean there wasn't an ulterior motive. "Thanks. You are …?" Why was a shifter, one who I didn't even know, bringing me food? Not that I was going to turn it down. It would save me the trouble of going back to the kitchen if I needed more calories to fuel my recovery.

He fidgeted under my scrutiny. "Jonah. Jonah McNeman."

"Well, Jonah. Thanks for the food." I set it inside my room on a nearby end table, but didn't bother to open the door farther or invite him in.

"If that's all, I need to clean up and…" I trailed off, not really sure how to tell him to go away now without being rude, but I waved my bandaged arm in front of myself grateful I had a legitimate excuse.

This was the third guy this week to randomly bring me food.

I wasn't complaining, but it was beginning to seem suspect. Maybe it was a weird shifter thing. I wasn't sure. Or maybe they knew I was grieving and just like I'd taken Marion a pie, they wanted to give me comfort food too?

He stood there for several moments, unsure of what to do next. He was definitely a submissive. Not that I was hating on him for it. It was just uncommon.

His full lips pressed into a thin line as I moved to close the door. "Wait." He put his hand out to stop me. "Is there anything I can maybe help you with?"

I quirked a brow. "Like what?"

"Your arm, it's still bleeding. Why don't you let me help you put on a clean bandage? That one looks…"

I lifted a brow. Yeah, it was shoddy at best, but Declan's shirt was working, for now. And there was no way in hell I was inviting a complete stranger into my room.

Was that his goal here? To get inside my private quarters?

"Jonah." A sudden growl came from the hallway. "What are you doing here?" At the sound of James's deep voice, my visitor stood up straighter, his expression growing wary.

"I'm being courteous and ensuring Aria is looked after." He kept his gaze on the ground.

Even I didn't buy that line. From the look on James's face, he wasn't buying it either.

I propped one hand on my hip, the other still holding my muffin. I took another bite as I watched their exchange with mild interest.

"She doesn't need you to look after her," James growled.

Oh, so we were getting all growly now, were we? This could get interesting. Too bad I didn't have any popcorn.

Jonah opened his mouth, as if to argue his point, but then promptly shut it and turned to leave.

Probably for the best. Though, I wouldn't have minded some entertainment to take my mind off my shoulder. It was throbbing.

I watched him retreat like a dog with his tail between his legs, and for a moment I felt bad for him.

That moment didn't last very long.

With him gone, James pushed his way into my room as if he owned it.

"Why yes, James, please do come in."

He grunted but didn't otherwise respond.

"So, tell me, why are random male Pack members going out of their way to see if I need help? Bringing me food, offering help I never asked for? Jonah is the third one this week."

Again, James made a noncommittal grunt before taking a seat on my bed and swiping a strip of bacon from the tray.

"Seriously, James, what gives?" My patience was running out after the day I'd had.

"They're courting you," he growled, obviously not thrilled with the idea.

Well, he could join the club. I wasn't thrilled by the idea either.

"Want to run that by me again?" I set my muffin down and folded my arms across my chest.

James shook his head, his brown hair falling in front of his face. "Look, they're trying to show you that they can provide for you. That they can keep you warm and safe and comfortable."

"You're kidding me?" My laughter filled the room. That was ridiculous. "Why? What could they possibly get out of it?"

"You're a beautiful woman, Ari. You can't blame them for trying."

Hmm, nice try. But I wasn't buying it. Shifters rarely went outside the pack to mate, and an unstable pyro with a bad attitude was hardly a prize.

There was something else going on.

"What aren't you telling me?" I asked.

The flash of guilt on James's face told me he was hiding something from me. He might know me better than most, but I knew him just as well.

In a flash, the expression was gone, and his face hardened as he tried to change the subject. "What happened outside of Sanborn Place today?"

"Don't change the subject, James. You're hiding something."

"I'm not hiding anything." His words were a snarl.

Whoa there, someone was having a temper tantrum. I resisted the urge to needle him further. His eyes had turned to silvery pools of liquid mercury, and he shot me a glare that screamed *back off.*

He was on edge today, and his wolf was riding shotgun.

I sat down in the lone chair and decided to just let it go for now.

James's shoulders relaxed, and he leaned back to rest against the headboard.

"Would you at least keep your shoes off the comforter?"

He kicked his boots off and folded his arms behind his head. "So, you going to tell me what happened, or should I just ask Declan?"

"Cut the crap, James. I know you already spoke to him or you wouldn't be here."

He shrugged his shoulders. His black tee stretched tight across his chest, highlighting the muscles hidden underneath.

I grabbed my half-eaten muffin from the side table and threw it at his head.

He caught it effortlessly, as though the damn thing moved in slow motion. He smiled wide as he took a bite, making a show of enjoying my snack.

Jerk.

"A newly turned vampire attacked like he was a heat-seeking missile, and I was his target. I have no idea why. But he had a photo of me in his pocket." I handed James the photo I'd found on the vampire.

His eyes hardened and his lips pressed into a thin line as he scrutinized it. "This is a recent photograph."

"I know. Based on the snow, it can't be more than a week or two old. After I lost Mike—" I paused as a wave of grief washed over me. Turning away from the look of pity on James's face, I closed my eyes and pushed down the pain, and frustration still haunting me.

"After I lost Mike, I thought killing the bastards responsible for his death would put an end to all of this—they'd come for me, I'd killed them, problem solved. But someone is still after me, and they obviously have vampire connections." I ran my fingers through my waist-length brown hair and quickly braided it to get it out of the way. "Rebecka can be ruthless, but she isn't stupid. With so few vampires surviving the transition, she wouldn't have created one only to throw him away. He was twenty-four hours old, at most. And he would have survived had he gone after easier prey. But he zeroed in on me. I don't think the Coven was involved." I sat back in my chair, my mind spinning over the possibilities.

"What if it was a rash attempt to get rid of you? You're their biggest threat."

I shook my head. "She knows I'm a pyrokinetic. It would take a lot more than a single fledgling to bring me down."

"True. Not her style." James nodded his head in agreement. "If Rebecka wanted you dead, you'd never see it coming."

James and I had done a fair amount of research on the Coven—and Rebecka, for that matter—to learn what made them tick.

Our motivations, however, had been different.

I'd looked into the Coven because they were one of three major players in the Pacific Northwest and knowledge was power.

James had done some digging because, despite the truce the two factions had with one another, the vampires were still his enemy.

"So, the question is… who's bold enough to go against Rebecka?"

Whoever it was, I needed to get to them before Rebecka did, or I'd have no remains left to question. Rebecka would see them as a threat to her position and authority. I was also almost certain that she knew I was a Friend-of-the-Pack.

Attacking me was like taking the first shot in battle. If the Pack discovered who was behind it, they'd be forced to respond. And I'd owe Declan yet another favor.

Rebecka wouldn't risk it. So, someone was either very sure of themselves or very stupid.

I was betting on stupid.

"This is exactly why I wanted to question the vampire that

attacked me. I can't believe Declan killed him." I balled my hands into fists.

"Ari, what did you expect him to do? The vampire had his fangs buried in you."

Urgh. Of course, Declan gave him all the details. I stood up and paced the floor. "I expected him to let me handle it. I'm a grown woman. I can take care of myself. Besides, it was just a little flesh wound."

James eyed my injured arm with narrowed eyes and growled deep in his chest as he rose from the bed. "He thought you were in trouble and needed help." He pulled my right arm away from my chest, exposing the DIY bandage.

He made a sound of disgust in the back of his throat before going to the attached bathroom and grabbing the first-aid kit under the sink. "Get in here. It needs to be cleaned or you'll get an infection."

I rolled my eyes but followed him inside anyway. "Vampires don't carry diseases," I reminded him.

He didn't answer, instead; he took my arm and peeled off the shirt, exposing the raw and angry wound beneath it.

I hissed as the fabric tugged at the jagged edges of the bite.

"It looks worse than it is, and I didn't need any help." I tried to pull my arm away, but James wasn't having it.

He turned on the faucet, waiting for the water to warm before cleaning the bite and re-bandaging it with fresh gauze.

"Thanks." I folded my arms over my chest and scowled at him. His expression was granite-hard, his eyes twin pools of silver. "What do you care, anyway? Why does it matter if I think Declan behaved like a complete moron without thought or consideration for the situation?" Because clearly, he had.

His growl deepened and small ripples spread across his arms beneath the surface of his skin. "I care because he's my Alpha. You should show some level of respect and you should stop trying to get yourself killed."

I scoffed. "Well, he isn't my Alpha, and he needs to stay the hell out of my way. Maybe then I can finally get some answers."

James stormed out of the bathroom. "Do you care that you could have been seriously injured? You're not indestructible, Ari."

"I'm not made of glass either."

He ran his hands through his dark brown hair, tugging at the ends in frustration. "Sometimes, I think you want to get hurt. You're reckless. When are you going to learn that it's okay for people to care about you? And when are you going to stop being so selfish?"

Whoa, where had that come from?

Without another word, James stormed out of my room, slamming the door behind him.

I shook my head and glared at the door. I should go after him. But what good would it do me? "Not like you'd apologize," I muttered, because let's be honest, I had nothing to apologize for.

I retrieved my messenger bag from the floor and pulled several files from its depths. James just needed some time to cool off. He'd get over it.

Sanborn Place was under construction, but I had a business to run and it didn't matter if I had an office to work out of or not. Everything had come to a screeching halt when Mike died, a month ago. It was time to get back to it.

I placed my hand on the pile of files on the bed and thought of Mike. He'd drilled into me the importance of thinking ahead, looking at all the angles, and always being prepared.

Which was why I'd always kept copies of my client files at home, just like he had. You could never be too careful.

I organized my files, along with the ones Marion had given me, and sorted them into three piles.

One pile was for repeat clients like Alexander Drucano. He often hired Sanborn Place for bodyguard details for his teenage daughter. And he was a client we could count on for repeat business.

The second pile was for clients I either didn't want to work with, or those I didn't think would hire me without Mike's presence.

And that was entirely okay by me. I was a one-woman show at the moment, so I couldn't carry all of our old clients anyway.

Most of the clients in pile number two were mages, and they tended to be a destructive and volatile lot. They could find someone else to save their asses when they summoned a demon too big for them to contain on their own.

The third pile was for prospects. I had five possible new clients lined up. Those who'd reached out to Sanborn Place within the last few months, but hadn't yet hired any of our mercs.

Our mercs. "Shit." I was going to have to figure out a way to hire people.

With any luck, Nico Salgado and Taylor Baired would come back, but I wasn't counting on it. Mercenaries were in high demand, and they'd gone without work from Sanborn Place for over a month.

They'd probably already moved on.

With a sigh, I dropped the rest of the papers on the bed and pulled my Pack and Coven files from between my mattress. It'd been risky bringing the Pack one into the Compound. If Declan found out I had it, I'd be dead meat, but I couldn't help myself. Information was power.

I'd learned a lot since I'd moved in, and I needed to make sure I recorded every detail. It'd be stupid not to.

I hastily wrote down Jonah McNeman's name and a brief physical description of the man. I didn't know what his beast was, let alone if he was anyone important. But it never hurt to have too much information.

I'd already recorded the names and attributes of each Alpha and higher-up shifter I'd come across so far. And took special care to record anything that stood out about them, like the fact that Robert Yazzie, the Canidae Clan Alpha, was freakishly good-looking but one scary as hell bastard that I avoided at every turn.

He was a tricky coyote. The type to smile right before he slit your throat.

I shivered. Good looks aside, he wasn't someone I wanted to walk into a dark alley with.

Just as I was putting everything away, tucking the Pack file back between my mattress and box spring for safekeeping, the hairs on the back of my neck rose.

I jerked my head around the room, looking for Inarus. He was here. I could feel it. Frantically, my gaze went over every corner of the room, but just as quickly as it had come, the sensation of not being alone left.

Urgh!

On the side table beside the serving tray of food was a single rose and a small envelope beside it. I stomped over to the table, my bare feet making muffled thumps on the carpet.

I hated that he could do that. That he could so easily teleport into the room and invade my space with no warning. It made me feel vulnerable and kept me on edge. Sometimes when I slept, I'd wake to the feeling of being watched. I never saw him, of course, not here at the Compound. And for all I knew, it was just a dream, my imagination. But I could never be sure.

I pulled the card from the envelope, ignoring the rose. I was beginning to hate roses.

I know who's after you. Meet me at the Ref tonight at nine o'clock and I'll explain.

I stared at the card for several minutes, chewing on his words. I searched for a double meaning, but couldn't find one.

If Inarus did, in fact, know who was out to get me, I needed that information. Meeting him tonight might be a risk, but I'd take my chances. Until I knew who my enemy was, I would be at a disadvantage. Even if Inarus was my enemy too.

I looked at the clock on the wall. It was only four o'clock. I had five hours to kill.

"Might as well make those client calls."

Chapter Four

At 8:15 I walked through the halls of the Compound and did my best to look inconspicuous.

Have I mentioned that I suck at being inconspicuous?

My boots thunked on the concrete floor with each step, and I inwardly cursed my inability to be as silent as a shifter. You'd think after spending so much time with them, I'd have picked up a trick or two.

I kept my eyes straight ahead and walked at a normal pace even though all I wanted to do was book it and get the hell out of dodge. My biggest worry was that I'd run into James or Declan. Neither would be happy about me sneaking out to meet with Inarus. Alone. Fortunately, both of them should be in their quarters, which were on the third floor.

Too bad my heart didn't know that. It still jumped in my chest every time someone rounded a corner or opened a door. At this rate, I'd have a heart attack before I left the building.

I wrung out my hands and flicked my gaze around as I turned the last bend in the staircase and finally hit the main floor, the exit clearly in sight.

Yes! Home free.

Just a little bit further.

It was almost too easy.

I reached for the door handle, but before my fingers could connect, Declan walked right through the front doors.

Shit.

I'd been so close. I groaned.

His eyes met mine, and he frowned, immediately suspicious.

Just my luck.

"Hi." I waved and tried to sidestep around him. With any luck, he'd let me pass. He had to know I was pissed at him for earlier. If he was like any normal guy, he'd let me go just to avoid a confrontation.

Unfortunately, he wasn't like every other guy.

"Where do you think you're going?"

"Out," I said and brushed past him.

Declan reached out and gripped my bicep. He really needed to stop touching me.

I turned to face him. A woodsy pine scent tinged with mint filled my senses. I started to lean in to inhale his scent deeper, but caught myself and jerked my head away.

Where the hell had that come from?

"That isn't a good idea. You were just attacked earlier today. You're not going anywhere. Not with the threat to you still out there and not when you should be resting."

Who the hell did he think he was giving me orders?

I shook him off. "Maybe if you hadn't killed the only viable source of information I had, I wouldn't need to go out right now."

His eyes narrowed, and I realized my mistake too late.

Stupid, Aria. Stupid, stupid, stupid. I wanted to bang my head into the nearby wall.

"And where exactly are you going?"

I folded my arms over my chest. "That isn't any of your business."

"I beg to differ."

I rolled my eyes and continued forward. Again, he stopped me, this time by stepping in front of me and blocking my path with the bulk of his body.

Declan stood at six feet tall, five inches over my five-foot-seven frame and tall enough that I had to look up in order to glare at him. It totally ruined the effect of my scowl when I had to look up.

He folded his arms across his chest, the forest green thermal shirt he wore stretching across his chest and shoulders. It drew my eyes to his well-defined muscles. Ropes of corded strength wrapped around him. He was imposing and sure, he was attractive, not that I would ever admit it out loud, but I refused to back down.

I got right in his face, drawing myself to my full height and then some as I stood on my tiptoes. "Look, you don't own me." I poked him in the chest with my index finger. "You don't control me, and you have no right to tell me what I can or can't do. You are not my mother or my father, and you certainly aren't my lover so get out of my way."

His furrowed brows cast shadows across his eyes, glinting metallic emerald in the bright entryway lights. I felt more than saw his tiger thrumming just beneath the surface, itching to take over.

My heart skipped a beat when a wide, feral smile suddenly spread across his face.

"What are you smiling about? I asked warily.

"So, if I was your lover you would obey my orders?"

I snorted. Not a chance in hell. I'd never obey anyone's orders, and I wasn't suicidal, so taking Declan as my lover was a hell no too.

Declan stepped forward, invading my space and forcing me to retreat back several steps. He prowled closer until I found my back pressed against a smooth stone wall, his eyes hooded.

Fire licked the exposed skin of my hands and forearms. A defensive reaction I had no control over.

His gaze flicked to the small flames before taking a single step back. There was no fear or concern in his gaze. No, the bastard looked amused.

I folded my arms over my chest and tried to slow my hammering heart. "Get out of my way." I put every ounce of haughty irritation into my voice that I could muster.

He flashed a feral smile. "You're kind of cute when you're angry."

He did *not* just call me cute.

I put my hands on my hips and rocked back on my heels. "Oh really? Well, I'm about to be fucking gorgeous here in two seconds."

That drew a laugh, deep and rich.

I gritted my teeth.

"You, little girl, are reckless, impulsive, and acting without regard for your own well-being. Now stop playing around and tell me where you think you're going."

Where did I think I was going?

Oh, I wanted to hit him. Really hard upside the head. Or maybe light his ass on fire. I smiled at the thought. He was so damn arrogant. Just one little fireball and—

Our eyes locked, and I was hit with the realization that I would lose. Damn Alpha stare. He wouldn't budge. The Alpha was too, well, Alpha.

Lighting his ass on fire still sounded like a good idea though.

Various scenarios played in my head as I tried to find a way around him. I needed to get to the Ref. I was already short on time as it was.

Knowing he'd scent a lie, I decided to be truthful. Well, mostly. I wouldn't lie. But I wouldn't give him everything either.

"Look, I'm going to the Ref," I said with a huff. "Will you let me go now?" The Ref was a well-known bar and grill in Spokane

Valley and had a reputation as an upstanding establishment. So really, Declan shouldn't have any reason to stop me from going. For all he knew, I just wanted to have a drink and forget about today.

He was skeptical, though. His nostrils flared, and I knew he was trying to detect whether or not I was lying.

I wasn't, and he knew it. He took a step to the side, and I was finally able to brush past him.

"Thank you," I said, keeping my nose high. It was about damn time. My flames receded as I opened the main door and stepped outside. I wanted to run, but I kept my steps even, my breathing light. I was outside, but I wasn't in the clear yet.

I walked down the stone pathway that led to my car. The outside air was crisp and light. It stung my cheeks as I neared my Honda Civic. A thin layer of frost covered the ground. I'd need to look at getting snow tires soon.

All of a sudden, the hairs on the back of my neck rose, and I felt the distinct sensation that I wasn't alone.

I turned around and dammit, there he was.

Declan was right behind me. Literally.

"What are you doing?" I halted my forward momentum and scowled.

"Coming with you."

I scowled harder. "No, you're not. I don't need a babysitter." When was he going to get that through his thick skull?

He shrugged his shoulders, unfazed.

I decided to ignore him and rounded to the driver's side. Opening the driver's side door, I slid inside and promptly hit the lock button.

Declan reached for the passenger handle and pulled on the door.

Locked. Just in time.

A smile tugged the corners of my lips, and I started the engine.

There was a knock on the window, and Declan indicated for me to open the door.

I shook my head. *Nope, not going to happen, buddy.* I put the car in reverse and gently pressed the gas.

The car didn't move.

I frowned. Pressing a bit more forcefully on the gas pedal, I tried again. Nothing.

I glared at him. His arm was braced on the car, one hand firmly holding onto the door handle.

I flipped him off and pushed the gas pedal harder. Smoke billowed behind my car. Then I heard a crunch of metal and watched wide-eyed as he casually tossed my passenger side door handle away.

What the hell? I took my foot off the gas and pressed the automatic button to roll down the window. The switch not moving nearly fast enough.

"What the hell is your problem?" I shouted.

His eyes twinkled with amusement before he reached through the window, lifted the inside door handle, opened the door, and proceeded to climb in the car. Calmly reaching for the seatbelt, he buckled himself in, sat back and looked as relaxed as ever.

The car continued to idle as I sat there fuming. I glowered at him as though I could will him to get the hell out of my car with just my gaze.

"Well, are we going?" he asked after a full minute had passed.

"No, we are not going. Get out of my car! I don't need you following me."

"I'm not following you. If it were that simple, I'd have taken my own car. I'm visiting. Being social. You should try it some time."

He was kidding, right? He had to be kidding.

Looking at his expression, I realized that no, he was not kidding.

I thunked my head against my steering wheel. *Could my day get any worse?*

Resigned, I drove out of the Compound and headed towards the Ref. I did my best to ignore Declan despite his attempts at conversation.

I was not in the mood to make nice. With any luck, I'd find a way to lose Declan once we arrived. Because if he saw Inarus, blood was going to spill.

Inarus had been responsible for a shifter woman's death. He'd staged an elaborate crime scene trying to make it look like a vampire and shifter had killed one another, and Declan wasn't the forgiving type—not when it came to his people.

I could only assume that Inarus's end goal had been to cause more friction—if not incite an outright war—between the Coven and the Pack. Luckily, the Pack had seen the crime scene for what it was and no additional blood was shed.

But they'd lost a Packmate that night. That wasn't something Declan or any other Pack member would turn a blind eye to.

Shifting in his seat, Declan turned to face me. He took a deep breath and leveled me with his gaze.

I eyed him warily through my peripheral.

"I'm sorry for being rash in my decision to kill the vampire." The look on his face was laughable. It was like he had to chew glass just to get the words out. "I saw his fangs in your flesh and..." He trailed off and a frown crossed his face. "And my beast didn't..." He seemed to struggle for a moment. A soft rumble filled the confined space of my Civic. Huffing out a breath, he finally finished, "I don't like seeing a woman hurt."

It was almost comical how painful it was for him to utter that apology.

"Thank you." This was just weird. I was pretty sure he was losing his marbles because this was way out of the norm for him. Declan didn't typically apologize. He was Alpha. He didn't need to say I'm sorry. Not to me, or anyone for that matter. At least, that was how the Pack would see it.

"You don't have to sound so skeptical."

"I'm not. You're just behaving strangely."

"How so?"

"Well, for starters, you broke my car, forced yourself on my trip, and then apologized for being rash. Does any of that seem normal for Declan, Alpha of the Alphas, to you?"

"I didn't break your car, I broke the handle, and that was your fault. I didn't rip it off. Your foot on the pedal did that."

"Same difference."

Declan shrugged like it was no big deal.

"And you apologizing. That is definitely not normal."

Declan nodded. "Fine. I'll give you that one."

Chapter Five

We made it to The Ref with only minutes to spare.

I anxiously scanned the parking lot for any sign of Inarus. Aside from two men smoking near the entrance, the lot was surprisingly deserted.

I opened my door and flicked a glance at Declan. "I'll be back. Wait here." My voice brooked no argument.

"Right," Declan said as he climbed out of the vehicle.

Sonova … could he ever listen?

I slammed my door and turned on him, unable to rein in my anger and impatience. "Can you for once just, I don't know, take direction? I don't want you interfering or scaring him off." I took a deep breath and willed myself to calm down. As the saying goes, you can catch more flies with honey than… well the point was, if I was nice maybe he'd do what I wanted. For once. I lowered my voice and spoke softly. "Just wait in the car, please." The last word was forced.

Declan raised a brow. "Who are you meeting? I was under the impression that you were coming to the Ref to hang out. Maybe let off some steam. I thought we were being social."

Shit.

Why did I keep shoving my foot in my mouth? I huffed out a breath. There was no getting around this. "No. You were being social. I'm meeting someone who has information about today's attack. It's not a big deal."

"You want me to wait in the car while you meet with a dangerous supernatural?" Declan's voice was casual, like he was repeating my dinner order. "After having just been attacked earlier this morning?"

Ah, there was that scary gleam in his eyes.

I shrugged my shoulders. "I'm not meeting with anyone dangerous. Besides, what makes you think he's a supernatural?"

His eyebrow arched even higher.

"Fine, he's a supernatural. So what?"

"How do you know that whoever you're meeting wasn't behind the attack? I can't imagine anyone would have any information unless they'd had direct involvement. This could be a trap."

Yeah. I'd thought of that too. Not that I'd tell Declan that. But I still had to take the risk. "I know the guy. It's okay."

"No, it's not okay. You're not being smart about this, Aria. And I'm not going to watch you stick your neck out for no good reason."

God, he was so infuriating. "You are not my keeper!" I was practically yelling, small waves of heat coming off of me and melting the snow around my feet. How many times did I have to remind him? I was perfectly capable of taking care of myself. I didn't need him acting like my father for Christ's sake.

I walked around the Civic and stopped in front of him, my hands propped on my hips. "Look, I don't work well with others—"

"You've got that right," he interrupted.

I bit my cheek to hold in my retort but gave him my best glare.

He quirked a brow, unfazed.

"Whatever you might think, Inarus isn't a threat to me, so if you're going to be stubborn and refuse to wait in the car, at least stay the hell out of my way."

"You're meeting with that damn psyker?"

Whoops. Probably shouldn't have mentioned him.

Declan's skin rippled, faint shadows crawling across it.

No. He could not shift. Not here.

I hadn't met his beast before, and I had no desire to do so now.

"Declan ..."

No answer.

His emerald eyes were filled with flecks of gold. His lip curled, displaying a hint of fang.

God dammit.

I cupped his face and forced him to meet my gaze. "Hey there ..." I cooed in what I hoped was a soothing voice. I was in uncharted territory here. I let instinct guide me. "There's no threat. We're safe. I'm safe. Come on back."

He held my gaze with his Alpha stare, and I fought not to look away. "Come on. Easy does it."

After a beat, he blinked and slowly pulled away from me. Without saying a word, he turned away and walked back to the passenger side door. With his back turned, he leaned against the Civic and waited.

I let out a sigh of relief as I walked towards the far end of the lot. Snow melted beneath my feet and made sloshing sounds with each step. I didn't bother to look over my shoulder to see if he'd changed his mind and decided to follow. If he did, I was just going to have to hit him. There was only so much a girl could take.

Reaching the far side of the parking lot, I leaned against the brick wall and set in to wait. Spokane was cold this time of year. Fall rains had quickly turned to winter snows. But we were still in that in-between stage. The newly fallen snow was quickly turning to slush on the roads, and I could already feel the moisture seeping into my steel-toed boots just from the short walk across the parking lot.

Curiosity finally won out as the minutes passed, and I couldn't help but smile at the sight of Declan. He stood still as a statue, leaning against the side of my car. Assuming we'd be "socializing" inside the Ref, he'd left the Compound without a coat.

Sucked to be him right now.

His gaze was transfixed by tonight's full moon. It didn't call to him. Not in the way stories depicted shifters. They felt no compelling urge to take their animal form during a full moon. Nevertheless, Declan appeared captivated by its presence. Maybe just because it was beautiful to behold? I wasn't really sure.

Time ticked by at a snail's pace.

Where the hell was Inarus?

I pulled out my cell phone and checked the time. Inarus was forty-four minutes late.

He wasn't coming.

I kicked clumps of snow in frustration as I hurried back to my car, irritated that I'd waited in the cold for almost an hour, only to be stood up like a prom date.

Declan watched with narrowed eyes as I approached, a predator focused on its prey. I'd almost reached my vehicle when the hairs on the back of my neck lifted. I slowed my steps and looked around the lot.

"What is it?" He'd managed to reach my side, his voice holding a thread of concern.

I waited, scanning the area for any sign of Inarus. The sensation that I was being watched persisted for a full two minutes, but I couldn't figure out where it was coming from.

Declan stood by in silence, doing his own visual scan of the area.

We both came up empty.

"He was here," I said.

"How do you know?"

I looked at him like he was a moron before I realized that telling him it was a gut feeling would make me look like the moron. "I just do."

When I pulled my keys from my pocket, Declan took the hint and returned to the car. I climbed in and stared at him through the passenger side window.

He was waiting—hands in his jean pockets—for me to open his door from the inside.

I debated whether or not to let him in. He'd broken the handle, the jerk. It would serve him right if I drove off and left him stranded here in the Ref's parking lot.

The scowl on his face told me he'd just read my mind.

I muffled a laugh with my free hand as I leaned over and pulled open his door.

Declan slid in smoothly, his expression far from amused.

I coughed to cover my laugh, put the vehicle into drive, and cranked on the heater.

Declan placed both his hands in front of the vents. "You did not just consider leaving me there." He said it as though it were a statement, not a question. But I decided to answer him anyway.

"I would never do something so childish to the Alpha of the Pacific Northwest Pack." Laying it on thick with the honorific, I filled my tone with all the false sincerity I was capable of.

If the furrow between his brows was any indication, he wasn't buying it.

Stopping at a red light, my pocket vibrated. I dug out my cell and accepted the call. "Naveed."

"I'm looking for Sanborn Place. The voicemail said to call this number?" His voice carried a thick Hispanic accent. Was English his second language?

I pulled the phone away from my ear and stared down at the caller I.D.

Marion must have changed the voice message for the office line. I certainly hadn't thought to. That woman thought of everything.

"You've called the right person." My voice sounded uncertain. Come on Aria. You're the boss. Start sounding like it. "What can I do for you?"

A job right now was just what I needed. I shoved my insecurities aside. It didn't matter how big or small the gig was. I needed to get back in the game. Hitting the gym or wandering around the Compound was getting old. This would give me something to do. But I was surprised I had potential business already. I'd only just started reaching out to former clients earlier today.

"I have a problem on my farm. Something is eating my goats."

Okay. Maybe I did care about the type of gig. Was he seriously calling me because an animal was attacking his goat herd?

I shook my head. Well, it was better than nothing.

"Sir, I'd be happy to help. But is it possible that a wild coyote is attacking your goats?"

"No, I've seen it with my own eyes. A monster haunts my lands."

From his opening statement, and now this, he sounded like an older man. A farmer who didn't have a lot of finesse when it came to talking to people.

He also sounded kinda fishy. Who said things like, "A monster haunts my lands?"

"*Ven.* I'll explain when you get here." He rattled off an address, and I tossed the notepad and pen I kept in the middle console to Declan.

I repeated the farm's address as it was given to me. Declan quickly jotted down the numbers then indicated, pen still in hand, for me to turn back the way we'd come.

"*Por favor apúrate.*" Please hurry.

I wasn't fluent, but I knew enough to get by with most Spanish speaking clients. I promised I'd be there within the hour. It wasn't like I had anything better to do. Turning my Civic around, I headed towards Green Bluff.

I offered to drop Declan off at the Compound on my way. Hell, I practically insisted. But he refused. I had a shadow tonight, and it didn't look like I'd be losing him anytime soon.

Chapter Six

We arrived at the Trezzi Farm out in Green Bluff a half hour later. The owner boasted ten acres of property in Spokane's local farming lands.

A large red barn greeted us as we pulled into the long dirt driveway, passing a small herd of goats and a cluster of chickens along our way. Their heads rose as we drove past, and they made anxious bleating sounds. It was like they sensed the predator in their midst.

Declan gazed out the window, a wry grin on his face.

When we parked, a Hispanic man in overalls came out of one of the three barns I'd spotted on the property to greet us.

"Miss Naveed?" he called and wiped his hands with a small red rag as he came towards us.

"That'd be me." I reached my hand out when I was close enough.

He put his hands up, showcasing his grease-covered palms. "Sorry, I haven't cleaned up, was working on my tractor."

I pulled my hand back and pointed toward Declan to make introductions. "No worries. This is my associate, Declan." I purposely omitted Declan's last name, which would have identified him as the Alpha of the Pacific Northwest Pack.

Most knew the Alpha by name, not by face.

Even though paranormals had come out of the closet during the Awakening six years ago, people were still skittish when faced with a shapeshifter. Given that a shifter could kill you without a weapon because hell, they were a weapon, I couldn't really blame them.

Mr. Ortiz appeared nice enough. But I didn't want to push his fear boundaries. He was already on edge about monsters lurking in the shadows.

Declan inclined his head in acknowledgment but didn't offer to shake Mr. Ortiz's hand.

"Please, come this way." Mr. Ortiz led us around the easternmost barn. The smell of motor oil was strong as we walked towards the small, but well-kept, home hidden behind it. And though it was dark, night having taken over, the property was well lit with pillar lights spaced periodically throughout.

We climbed the three-step porch and took a seat on the outdoor furniture. I reclined in a wicker chair. Declan claimed a seat beside me with Mr. Ortiz across from us.

"Can I get you anything to drink?" he asked.

"No, thank you. Why don't you just dive in and give us the details?"

He nodded his head before scanning the darkened horizon. His hands nervously fiddled with the watch at his wrist.

I rocked back and forth in the wicker rocking chair, allowing the motion to relax my muscles as I waited for Mr. Ortiz to start. The desperation and fear emanating from him told me he needed time to tell his story. Whatever he was about to say was clearly difficult for him.

Declan sat motionless beside me, though his eyes never left Mr. Ortiz's face, and his nostrils kept flaring. Was he scenting Mr.

Ortiz's fear? Or was that just a weird habit of his I hadn't noticed before?

"A creature has been killing my *ganado*. My goats." His voice was a hushed whisper, as if this supposed creature might hear him.

"A creature?" I was going to need him to be a tad more specific. There were several breeds of creatures out and about these days.

He nodded. "Where I come from, this creature is a myth. A legend told from generation to generation to keep our children in line. But it is real, and it is here. I have seen the *monstruo* with my own eyes." He shivered and rubbed his hands over his worn blue jeans. "It was tall. Nearly nine feet with a hunched back. It had leathery skin and razor spikes running down its spine." His eyes widened as he described the creature to us. His fear was palpable.

Whatever he'd seen, it had scared the hell out of him. Nine-foot-tall creatures with spikes down their back and leathery skin weren't something I'd heard of before. Part of me wondered if perhaps he'd stumbled upon a shifter in their between form. A blend between human and shifter that often made them twice as large and twice as scary. If he'd seen one at night, it wouldn't be unheard of for his imagination to exaggerate what he was seeing. Convincing him that the monster before him was the monster he'd grown up fearing as a child.

"Do you know what it was?" I was curious as to the name of this mysterious monster. If it was one from old legends, then it had to have a name.

He nodded, running his hands through his graying hair and looking everywhere but at me. I could tell he didn't want to say it aloud. I wondered if it was like saying "Voldemort." Would it magically appear?

I waited until he was ready.

Seconds passed, turning into minutes until finally, he released a defeated breath. "*La Chupacabra*," he whispered.

I barely made out the words, but when I did, I had to fight the snort that wanted to escape.

He had to be kidding. The idea that he'd seen a shifter in a between form was becoming more and more likely by the second. But this was a job, so I'd play my part, confront the shifter if he came back, and collect my paycheck.

As Mr. Ortiz continued to speak, explaining in detail how he'd watched the Chupacabra slaughter several of his goats, I watched Declan from the corner of my eye. If the person behind the goat slaughter wound up being a shifter, I wondered how he would handle it. He ran the Pack with an iron fist. Reckless, aggressive behavior of this caliber was unacceptable. It also served to fuel the fear and negativity that humans still held onto towards shapeshifters. Declan would be forced to take action. And it wouldn't be pretty.

"How many attacks have you seen?" I sat forward and threaded my fingers together.

"There have been three." He paused and looked out toward the fields. "But I have only witnessed one. One was enough." His hands shook as he rubbed his palms on the front of his jeans again.

"What did the monster do with the animals after it killed them?" Declan asked.

I gave him a hard stare. What the heck kind of question was that? Did it matter what the creature did with the dead animals?

Mr. Ortiz seemed to think it was a completely rational question, though, because he didn't even hesitate with his response. "It bit into their necks and sucked the blood from their bodies until they were bled completely dry. Then," He shrugged his shoulders. "It moved on."

That didn't sit right. Shifters did attack animals in their beast forms, but they wouldn't suck them dry of blood. That was more of a vampiric behavior. But vampires didn't look like animalistic monsters, and they didn't consume animal blood.

At least, not that I was aware of. I supposed if a vampire was starved enough they may drink animal blood, but that still didn't explain the physical description.

"Did you keep any of the bodies?" I asked.

He nodded and rose from his seat, leading us around the home to one of the barns we'd passed earlier. Behind it was a shallow ditch, haphazardly dug from the looks of it.

I pulled out my cell phone. Utilizing the flashlight feature, I illuminated the ground around us. The smell of decaying flesh hit me hard as we drew close to the ditch, and I wrinkled my nose as I peered over the edge.

I covered my mouth and nose with my free hand to keep from breathing in the stench and fought to hold back the vomit threatening to escape.

I failed miserably.

Turning away, I placed my hands on my knees and retched up the contents of my stomach. Good thing I'd only eaten the muffins.

Breathing hard, I wiped my mouth on the back of my hand and stood up on shaky legs, using a nearby apple tree for support. The two men beside me looked anywhere but at me as I pulled myself together.

"You okay?" Declan asked when I neared.

I nodded and swallowed, my throat burning. "Just peachy."

I held my phone high once again and scrutinized the remains, ignoring the discomfort I felt. Resting atop one another, there looked to be at least seven goat corpses.

Mr. Ortiz hadn't been lying when he'd said they'd been bled dry. They looked like husks of their former selves.

I considered taking a closer look.

But I really didn't want to.

I crouched down, steeling myself and preparing to hop into

the ditch, when Declan launched himself over the edge in a graceful pounce. He landed on the balls of his feet beside the bodies, the smells seemingly having no affect on him. Though I knew that couldn't be true.

I looked to Mr. Ortiz, shrugging my shoulders to his unspoken question, and waited while Declan took a closer look.

He crouched down low on his haunches as he peered at the bodies, moving their heads this way and that.

"Find anything interesting?" I asked.

He shook his head. After a few more minutes of poking and prodding, he reached up and used a tree root from the nearby apple tree to pull himself out of the ditch without ruining his clothing or appearing too shifter like.

As he crested the top, I scrutinized his expression to decipher how he was managing to deal with the cloying scent of death. His eyes were glossy, but that was the only indication that the smell was getting to him. Given his enhanced shifter senses, I was surprised he could come within fifty feet of the bodies.

"You were right when you said they'd been bled dry," he commented. "They're little more than skin and bones at this point, but aside from the lack of blood, nothing seems overly unusual about their deaths. If I didn't know better, I'd say they were attacked by wolves or coyotes based on the claw and bite marks. Natural ones would have been my first guess, but there isn't anything natural about this." He paused and pressed an index finger to his chin. "An animal wouldn't have left the flesh intact. They would have eaten the meat, not wasted it. A shifter would have done the same. These,"—he indicated the goat bodies below—"don't smell right." He wrinkled his nose in a gesture of disgust before looking away.

There was something he wasn't saying, but I'd ask him about it later. Whatever his reason for silence, it was likely a good choice.

"What do you mean when you say they don't smell right?"

Mr. Ortiz asked. His voice was even, but his eyes were wide, as though he already knew the answer.

With a slight incline of his head, Declan offered a casual smile, then loped off towards the car, leaving me alone with Mr. Ortiz.

"He's a shifter," Mr. Ortiz said with a hard swallow. It wasn't a question.

"He is. You just had the pleasure of meeting Declan Valkenaar, the Alpha of the Pacific Northwest Pack." I watched as panic filled his eyes. But it disappeared just as quickly as it arrived.

I was impressed. It wasn't every day that, unbeknownst to him, a human farmer found himself in the company of a shapeshifter. Let alone the Pack Alpha. Mr. Ortiz handled it very well.

"I suppose I should be grateful that he came and checked things out," he said finally.

I nodded in agreement. I knew just as he did that had Declan even scented a shifter in the area or that if this had been a shifter attack, he would have taken immediate measures.

"Did you notify the Human and Paranormal Enforcement Division?"

"The HPED?" He spat out a tobacco chew and made a sound of disgust. "*Sí*. They said they could not help. They wouldn't even come out here to investigate. It wasn't their problem. *Inútil*." Useless.

It figured. The HPED only responded to human-related issues. A monster hunting down Mr. Ortiz's herd didn't exactly qualify as a human problem.

Until a human death resulted from whatever was attacking the goats, the HPED wouldn't get involved. They weren't all that concerned with preventative measures.

"Why don't I stay here for a few days and see what I can come up with? If this monster comes back, I'd like to be on site."

He nodded. "You can stay in the barn if it suits you."

It didn't. But I couldn't stay in his home. Safe and sound, tucked away in a house, I'd miss all the action as well as any noises that could alert me to an intruder. So, the barn it was.

He led me back the way we'd come and showed me inside the first barn we'd passed while driving up. It was surprisingly clean and thankfully didn't appear as though any of the animals slept inside. Most of the enclosure was filled with hay, farming tools, and seed. More of a storage barn than anything. I had to assume it was insulated since it was noticeably warmer inside.

At least I wouldn't freeze at night.

In the back corner was an unused horse stall, the majority of it packed with piles of hay.

"It isn't luxurious, but with some blankets, the hay piles will make a soft bed."

I nodded. It would do.

I told Mr. Ortiz that I'd be back in an hour or two. I needed to retrieve some personal belongings if I was going to be staying out here, and I needed to get rid of Declan.

I wasn't surprised when Declan pulled me aside as soon as I reached my car. "Whatever did that," he said, waving his arm in the direction I'd come from, "Isn't an animal I've ever come across before."

I shrugged my shoulders. "After the Awakening, anything is possible. Does it really matter that this is something you haven't seen before?"

"I've been around a long time. Longer than it would appear."

I knew that already. Shifters had longer lifespans than humans. So, while Declan appeared to be in his early thirties, he was probably older.

"I won't allow you to stay out here alone. It's too dangerous." Declan's strong arms were folded across his chest, highlighting the bulge of his biceps. His frown was illuminated in the moonlight, and something inside of me really wanted to just hit him.

I got that urge more and more these days.

"Thanks for your concern, but I can take care of myself. And I don't need your permission to do my job." I had a business to run, and this was a paying gig.

"Aria, you're out of your league. I'll make arrangements for one of my men to ..."

"No. Absolutely not." I'd tolerated Declan and his insistence on babysitting my every move lately, but I was drawing the line. "Get in my way here, and I'm out. You do not get to control my life." I walked to the driver side door. "This is where I draw the line, Declan. Accept it or I'll pack my bags and move out tonight."

His nostrils flared.

Ha! Scent the truth in that, asshole.

Chapter Seven

That night, crickets chirped, and the wind whispered its secrets, but there was no sign of any monster.

I'd spent most of the night wide-awake, expecting the slaughter that my mind conjured up every time I closed my eyes. When morning arrived, announced by the crowing of a rooster— that I really wanted to shoot, since I hadn't had my morning coffee—my eyes closed and my body relaxed into a restful state of sleep.

Mr. Ortiz didn't bother me until noon. A fact I was grateful for.

He entered the barn with a tray of food that smelled like heaven just after noon but despite the aroma, I couldn't muster up an appetite. "It isn't much, but I figured you'd be hungry. I'd have brought food sooner, but it didn't look like you were awake yet."

I eyed the tray wishing I could dig right into the chicken pot pie with enthusiasm but just thinking about eating made my stomach want to revolt.

He'd brought along some hot cocoa, which I drank as though I were a twelve-year-old child. It wasn't coffee, but it would do.

I spent the afternoon wandering around the farm.

A broken sea of clouds gave just enough cover from the sun's harsh rays. The chill was gone from the air, so I left my heavy coat in the barn, choosing to wear a pair of jeans, my black leather boots, and a cowl neck sweater. No snarky T-shirt today.

Even though Trezzi Farm wasn't too far from town, the closest neighbor was still several miles away. I'd forgotten how much I missed this way of life. I'd grown up in the middle of nowhere, much like this. My family had owned forty acres. No neighbors as far as the eye could see. It'd been quiet. Peaceful. We hadn't raised any animals. Or any crops for that matter. I think my Papa had just liked the solitude of it all.

But six years ago, when I was only seventeen, men dressed in black from head to toe invaded my home. And they had murdered my Papa in front of me.

I'd tried to fight the men off. I'd tried using my pyrokinetic abilities to save my parents' lives. But I'd been too young. Too unskilled. And they'd been so damn strong.

Tears formed in the corners of my eyes, and I swiped them away. I needed to shake off the memories of that night. I didn't want to see the light fading from my Papa's eyes. Or hear my mother's screams right before they were suddenly cut out. Leaving only the sound of the crackling flames and my labored breathing behind.

I'd never get over losing my parents, but I had good memories too.

My mind wandered to last month when everything I believed shattered in one night. The night I saw my mother alive and well, standing at the podium as she spoke to members of the Human Alliance Corporation.

Anger blossomed in my chest. "Six years," I growled. For six years I'd been alone. I'd believed she was dead. But in one night, I'd not only realized she was alive and had left me by choice, but Mike was murdered and Inarus's betrayal was brought to light.

I'd lost so much that night. But what hurt most of all was losing the illusion that my mother could have ever loved me.

The Human Alliance Corporation, or HAC for short, was an organization hell-bent on restoring their way of life pre-Awakening. Which meant getting rid of paranormals and anyone *other*.

Anyone like me.

Guess mommy dearest loved her ideals more than she loved her daughter. I kicked a clump of dirt before I climbed on top of a bale of hay and stared out at the horizon. This was like a Jumper movie remake only I was the main character in this B-rated film.

I hadn't confronted her yet. I wasn't sure I even wanted to. Did it matter what her reasons were for leaving me? "Nope."

A sickening feeling hit me in the gut. Was it possible she'd been involved with my Papa's death? I shook my head. She'd loved him, right?

There was no real way to know. And I would only drive myself crazy by trying to figure it out.

After spending the day plagued by memories of my childhood, I desperately hoped this mysterious monster showed its face tonight. I needed an excuse to fight something. Anything.

Hours ticked by, and boredom set in. Mr. Ortiz didn't speak to me for most of the day. He busied himself with his work on the farm and I wandered the grounds in an attempt to look busy.

I was grateful when nightfall came.

I'd just situated myself on my makeshift bed in the barn when the now familiar sensation of not being alone struck me. I kept as still as I could and waited to see if he would show himself. Inarus's usual MO was to teleport in, drop something off, and leave. Maybe he'd stick around this time.

I was spoiling for a fight.

The barn was cloaked in shadows. But there was still enough

light for me to make out his silhouette a few feet away—tall, broad-shouldered, casual stance.

"What do you want?" I got to my feet as though I didn't have a care in the world. Dusting my hands on my jeans, I faced him.

He stepped out of the shadows. A sliver of light washed across his face, illuminating his grey-blue eyes and the dusting of a five o'clock shadow along his chiseled jaw.

Before he could say a word, I reached for one of the daggers strapped to my thigh and threw it.

I aimed for his heart. But, as I'd expected, he ported, and my dagger embedded itself in the wood frame surrounding the doorway.

He ported back less than a second later, this time beside me. One of his arms snaked around my waist, and the other quickly grabbed my right wrist before I could draw another blade.

"Why are you always trying to kill me?" he asked, his voice a caress along my senses.

I shivered. "Because I really don't like you." I jerked away from him, taking a deep breath as I put space between the two of us.

The earthy clean smell of rainstorms assailed my senses. It was a scent I'd come to associate with him.

God. Wasn't that just great?

"I'm not your enemy."

"Yeah. You are, Inarus. What are you even doing here?" I put a hand up, halting him before he came any closer. Whenever he touched me, my mind went a little foggy. I had to remind myself more than I liked to that he wasn't one of the good guys. Not by a long shot.

He heaved a long-suffering sigh and ran his hand through the thick, black tendrils of his hair. It'd grown since the last time I'd seen him. "Do we need to get into it right now?"

Of course we did. Sometimes he was just so dense. He'd

betrayed me, used me like some pawn in his game. His audacity was astounding.

I could feel the rush of heat as my fire bubbled beneath my skin, encouraging me to let it out to play. It was a tempting thought, but not with the dozens of hay piles in the barn. I'd end up lighting the place up like a Christmas tree with just one stray spark. I sighed in resignation. No burning Mr. Tall, Dark, and Handsome. At least not today.

"Look, I didn't come to fight. I came to warn you."

"Like the other night at the Ref when you were a no show? I waited an hour for you in the cold. So thanks, but no thanks."

A small frown marred his near-perfect features as he stepped forward, then caught himself. I watched as he chose his next words carefully. "You weren't alone."

I narrowed my eyes at him. "You never said that I had to be."

He paced back and forth, clearly agitated. "Look, can we not argue? This is important."

I threw my hands up. "Fine, whatever. Why are you here? Tell me whatever is it that's so damn important."

He frowned at me. Yeah, I was still being a bitch, but I didn't care. I was working. This wasn't the time for idle chit-chat. Besides, I wasn't entirely sure I even wanted to hear what he had to say.

Okay, so maybe I wanted to hear what he had to say, but I didn't have to admit it to him.

Inarus paced over to a wooden barrel and leaned against it. His eyes tracked me for a few more seconds. I could see him debating whether to tell me whatever it was he had to say, or just port out and leave me on my own.

I wasn't sure which outcome I was hoping for.

"I was telling the truth when I told you I had nothing to do with that little boy's death."

Oh, you have got to be fucking kidding me. My vision went red.

Daniel Blackmore's death would always be a sore spot for me.

I'd been hired to find the seven-year-old boy, but I'd been too late. I still wasn't certain who was responsible for his senseless death, but I had a few ideas. One of which was the HAC's involvement. And I knew that Inarus worked with them.

That was enough for me. He may not have murdered that little boy with his own hands, but he was still culpable as far as I was concerned. "You have no right..." My hands shook at my sides.

"Aria, hear me out."

"Hear you out? HEAR YOU OUT?" I sucked in a lungful of air and forced my feet to take me outside. Flames licked my fingertips. I had to get away from the barn.

The brisk night air did nothing to temper my fiery anger as I whirled on him.

"You were involved—"

"I wasn't. I'd never condone the murder of a child. Had I been aware of their intentions—"

"You would have done what?" I wanted to shake him. I'd had nothing but time since Mike's murder. And I'd used it to research the HAC and dig up every shred of information I could find on them and the elite assassins who worked for them. Psykers who'd pledged their loyalty to the PsyShade and who operated within the HAC. Psykers like Inarus.

My bitter laugh echoed through the night.

"Aria. Please." His jaw was set in a firm line, but his eyes pleaded with me to understand.

I couldn't. "You killed an innocent vampire and shifter."

At my accusation his jaw hardened even more. "It couldn't be avoided."

"Her name was Emma. Did you know that?"

Regret flashed across his face.

"She was twenty-two. She had her whole life ahead of her."

"I—"

"Deny having any responsibility for Daniel's death all you

want. But you're sure as hell going to own Emma's and the unknown vampire. You murdered them in cold blood. Own it."

Eyes cast downward, he nodded.

"I know it won't absolve me in your eyes." He avoided my gaze. "But I know who killed the boy."

I stared down at my hands and watched the flames climb over my fingers and onto my palms.

"Did you hear what I said?"

Anguish filled me as my mind went back to the day I'd found Daniel's body. Broken and discarded like he was trash.

"Aria?"

"Who?" My fire burned bright and hot around me. All I needed was a name. And I would make them burn.

"Irina Petrova."

My head snapped in his direction. "Rebecka's second in command?"

He nodded. "She's been working with…" He paused and his lips thinned before he continued. "Viola has been in frequent contact with the vampire. I don't know the details, but Irina appears to be an asset."

He didn't look like he approved.

I'd known the HAC was involved, but knowing that my mother was at the head of all of this was another stab to my already wounded heart. "Why? Why would a vampire work with the HAC? What does she have to gain?"

He stepped closer, and I forced myself not to retreat. I needed to know what was going on. With a deep breath, I pulled my fire inside myself.

Inarus reached for my hand and threaded his fingers with mine. "She believes Viola and the HAC can help her eliminate the shifters."

"She's an idiot." I stared down at our hands. I was an idiot, too, for allowing this.

Inarus nodded. "Your mother will betray her the first chance she gets. But for now, she's serving a purpose."

"Because if the vampires and shifters war with one another—"

"The victor will be too weak to defend themselves when we attack."

"We?" I pulled my hand free from his and crossed my arms over my chest. My upper lip curled in disgust.

"Psykers are being recruited. We're training for battle. We all feel the war coming."

"I won't let it happen."

"And if you can't stop it?" he asked. "Will you let the shifters use you? Become their weapon of destruction against your own people?

I shivered at the thought. I was no one's weapon. "It won't come to that." I needed to find Irina. If I could get to her, all of this would go away. Rebecka would never work with the HAC. Irina had to be acting behind her back. And if I could prove it, Rebecka would end her.

And if I couldn't, I'd end her myself—consequences be damned.

"You can't strike her alone."

I didn't bother answering. I still wasn't sure if Inarus was friend or foe. Why had he given me any of this information? Was he trying to lure me into a trap? Or was he genuinely willing to help me?

He cupped my face in his warm, calloused palms. "If you go after her, I'm coming with you."

I shook my head. "I work alone. I won't have someone watching my back that I don't trust."

Pain flashed across his face before he hid it. "Then let me earn your trust."

I chewed on my lower lip. He was still the only other psyker I knew. And my pyrokinetic abilities had grown. Had become more volatile. If I could trust him in this, then maybe I could trust him to help me train. To learn better control. "I'll take it into consideration."

"Thank you… There's something else you should know."

I waited.

"The boy's parents were involved."

I sucked in a breath. "All of them?"

"Not the biological father. But his mother and her husband assisted in the abduction."

Rage unfurled in my gut. I'd believed them when they'd said they'd loved Daniel. I'd believed that they'd wanted him found and returned safely. They'd played me.

"I don't think Jessica Blackmore knew how far things would go. She'd agreed to the abduction under the ruse that the shifters would be blamed and he would eventually be returned. That wasn't the case."

No. It wasn't. "And her husband?"

"I wasn't involved in that mission. But Patrick Blackmore is a prominent member of the HAC. And the boy's murder and HAC involvement are no longer being kept secret."

I swore under my breath. I'd had my suspicions about the parents. Neither Patrick Blackmore nor Daniel's mother Jessica had seemed overly upset by their child's death when James and I questioned them, but to have played a role… How could they live with themselves?

"Patrick offered his stepson up as a sacrifice for the cause."

Jesus Christ. I'd hunt him down and take that bastard out myself.

"How do you know this?" I asked.

"You're going to have to take my word for it."

A goat baaaaaed in the distance. "You should go. I'm on a job." I had a lot on my mind, and I needed to be alone to sort all of it out.

"He's dead. Don't waste your time looking for him."

"What?" I snapped in surprise.

"Jessica murdered her husband before committing suicide."

I covered my mouth with my hand. Good riddance. That alleviated some of the problem. But I would still have Irina to contend with. "Okay. Thanks for the information. But you still need to go."

He frowned. I could tell he didn't want to leave. "I know this is none of my business. I won't try to control you but… Promise you'll be careful?"

I nodded.

"I know you don't trust me right now. I'm going to fix that," he said. And then he vanished. Only after he left did I realize he never told me what he knew about the baby vamp attack.

Chapter Eight

A shrill scream pierced the evening air. It jerked me from my slumber as effectively as a shot fired.

In an instant, I was on the move. Jumping from my bed of hay, I shoved my feet into my boots and pounded my way out of the barn.

Another scream gave me a location.

I turned to my left and ran. As I neared the tree line, the scream died away, replaced with the sickening sound of gurgles and slurps.

My skin crawled, and my stomach twisted with dread. Whatever animal had made that blood-curdling scream was dead now, and the monster that had attacked it was enjoying its meal with vigor.

A dark shape—nine feet tall and at least four feet wide—was barely discernible within the shadows.

Mr. Ortiz hadn't been exaggerating.

I slowed my steps, hunched down, and moved closer. Careful to remain silent and out of the creature's line of sight.

A twig snapped beneath my boot, and I froze.

The monster's head jerked up, and blood-red eyes met mine.

I tightened my grip on my daggers and held my breath as I waited to see how it would react to my presence. My heart hammered in my chest and urged me to run. But I knew from hanging around shifters that that was the worst thing I could do in this situation.

If I ran, I was prey. And prey was hunted.

It stepped forward from the brush and rose to its full, massive height.

Now I definitely wanted to run.

Before logic could guide me, the monster let loose a vicious cry and barreled towards me.

Fuck it.

I ran.

Instinct kicked in, and I hightailed it as fast as my legs would take me—twigs and frost crunching beneath my feet. My mind rushed for a solution on how to take the monster down and came up blank.

Fear suffocated my abilities to call my fire.

I could hear its thundering footsteps, and I chanced a glance behind my shoulder to see how far it was.

That was a mistake. As soon as I turned, my boot twisted in a tree root hidden beneath the blanket of snow, and I tumbled to the ground. My ankle wrenched from the fall. I twisted in an effort to roll to my feet, but I wasn't fast enough.

A massive paw swiped at my back, sending me sailing through the air and into the tire of a tractor nearby. The impact jarred me. My ribs protested, and I prayed nothing was cracked.

My vision blurred as I tried to regain my senses.

A door opened in the distance. I blinked multiple times, and Mr. Ortiz's form came into focus, illuminated in the doorway of his home.

Shit! His porch light cast a clear target for the monster to hone in on.

"Chupacabra!" I shouted.

Horror stamped across his face. The monster's gaze turned toward Mr. Ortiz, and I saw it ready itself to strike.

I couldn't let that happen. "Get inside!" I staggered to my feet. "Hey, you ugly sonavabitch! Over here!" I waved my arms in the air.

Its blood-red eyes narrowed on me.

"That's right. I'm right here. Come and get me."

I ran. But not before I shouted, "Call the Pack!" to Mr. Ortiz. Hopefully he'd heard me before slamming his door shut.

Declan had given him his card. With any luck, he'd hung onto it because I would need back up. I'd rather he called James, but I wasn't in a position to rattle off phone numbers or be picky.

As I ran, I focused on my hands, calling my fire to me. It took a few seconds, but it came. And before the Chupacabra could get any closer, I pivoted on my heel and rushed it.

Flames licked my arms. The space between us disappeared faster than I was comfortable with. When we were inches from colliding, I slid to my knees and bowed my back towards the ground as he sailed over me. Jumping to my feet, I turned and ran at his back before I launched myself onto it. My hands held onto the scales that covered its spine.

They'd looked grey from a distance, but they had a metallic green sheen to them up close. I dug my hand beneath them in search of softer flesh to hold as I blasted my fire into the creature's back.

It had little effect, but the creature now knew I was there.

It bellowed in rage and twisted back and forth trying to buck me off. I stabbed my daggers into the hard plates that armored its body and tried to anchor myself in place.

Forced to abandon my fire, I stabbed my second dagger in over and over, trying to hit something vital.

"Dammit. Why aren't you bleeding?" I gritted my teeth before I wrenched both daggers free and jumped to keep from being thrown off.

I landed in a crouch. "Come on, you bastard." I didn't know if it could understand me, but I needed to lead it away from the house. We were getting too close.

It huffed, spittle flying free from its maw as it roared once more and displayed an impressive expanse of double-rowed teeth, each sharp and deadly.

"You better not bite me, buddy."

This close I could see its leather-skinned underbelly and the thick fur that coated its arms and legs. It had a face like a wolf, and three-inch-long claws jutted out from each one of its fingers. Add that to the armored plates on its back and horned spikes down its spine, and it was one ugly bastard.

My eyes zeroed in its fur-covered limbs. Fur caught fire easily enough.

I pushed my flames out once more, molding my hands before me in the shape of a ball as the monster watched transfixed.

Spending precious seconds funneling my energy into the ball of fire, I made it as hot as I could before the beast lost interest and charged.

I let the flames free, directing the ball of fire to its left calf.

The smell of burnt hair was instant, and the monster roared in pain before rearing back to swipe at me.

I turned and ran as I tried to come up with a plan.

Fire glowed behind me as I raced through the fields, jumping over rocks and logs along my way.

It was still burning, but the monster wasn't going down.

A tractor sat about fifteen yards to my left, and I turned for it, adding a burst of speed to give myself the time I needed to climb it.

Almost there.

I hastily climbed on top of it and turned just in time to see the Chupacabra reach its claws out to strike me.

I launched off the tractor and dove over the monster. My feet cleared its shoulder as I sailed past, but not before one of its claws hit its mark and dug into my thigh.

I screamed. The sound echoed through the night, morphing into a battle cry as I turned, twisting my body and digging my blade into its back. "Take that, fucker!" My momentum carried me around and my blade dug a path through its scales. *Shit. Too shallow.*

No blood. Dammit. Come on!

Feet now on the ground, I jerked my blade free and twisted around.

My steps faltered. Blood soaked my jeans and ran down my thigh.

This wasn't good.

The ground rushed toward me. "Do. Not. Pass. Out."

The Chupacabra's roar made my heart race that much more. Adrenaline pumped through my veins and blocked out most of the pain. But for how much longer, I didn't know.

My fire didn't seem to have any effect. And my blades weren't doing much better. The monster's back was too heavily armored. But if I attacked its front, I would put myself at too great a risk.

Come on, Ari. Think of something, or you're going to die.

Chapter Nine

Dark spots coated my vision. I rubbed at them, but it was no use. My vision refused to clear.

Sweat dripped down my brow, and my leg was numb, all but dragging behind me as I struggled to stay ahead of the monster.

I couldn't stop moving.

To stop was to die.

I'd moved away from the open fields and into the surrounding evergreens. The trees acted as a thin barrier between me and the beast, but they were slowing me down as much as they slowed it down.

Bark embedded itself in my nails. Branches stuck in my hair. And sleet fell from the sky, coating the forest floor in a thin sheet of ice.

My boot slipped. I caught myself just before my face collided with the hard surface of a rock.

Tires crunched in the distance, and I tasted the first breath of hope since facing the monster.

A vehicle parked close to where I stood, its headlights spearing through the trees.

The Chupacabra had backed me into a corner. A stream stood

down a steep incline at my back, thick foliage on either side of me, and the monster in front.

I didn't think I could make it down to the stream, let alone cross it. My leg was barely holding me up as it was.

A wolf howled in the distance, and the monster snapped its head around, listening. With its eyes off me, I inched to my left as I tried to step around the brush without getting closer to the monster.

Another wolf howled, this one much closer.

I released a relieved breath.

Help had arrived.

Thank God.

The damn thing had gotten multiple hits in. In addition to my wounded leg, I sported a gash across my cheek and a deep laceration along my side. With so much blood loss, I wouldn't be surprised if I kissed the ground soon.

Two wolves exploded through the trees and launched themselves at the monster—each in varying shades of auburn—followed by a coyote that looked familiar.

It had to be Robert, the Alpha for Clan Cadinae.

James and Declan brought up the rear, both still in their human forms.

"He didn't have anything better to do?" I asked, my breaths labored as I indicated the coyote.

James flashed a grin. "You didn't think Robert would miss out on all the fun, did you?"

He was an idiot if he thought this was fun.

I leaned my body against a tree as renewed relief washed over me.

It didn't last long.

The wolves attacked in unison, each rending big chunks of flesh with their teeth and claws, but the monster refused to go down.

Robert chose speed and stealth. He leapt at the monster, sank his fangs into its flesh, and quickly retreated to safety. He did this again and again, trying to bleed the monster out.

I shook my head. "It won't work," I said. Not that he could hear me.

"What the hell is that thing?" Worry colored James's voice.

"Chupacabra—"

Declan turned glowing eyes on me. "It's real?"

Before I could respond, a yip drew our attention back to the fight. The wolves and Robert were on the defensive.

Fuck.

The monster was winning.

I pushed away from the tree and took a step forward. I couldn't just stand here and do nothing.

A hand on my arm stopped me.

"No." James shook his head. "You're too weak. Stay here."

James didn't bother to wait and see if I'd listen before taking off at a sprint. Declan was right behind him. They shifted to their between forms, their hands morphing into fur covered paws with claws sprouting from their tips. Declan's arms sheathed themselves in snow-white fur broken up by jet-black stripes.

If I wasn't so dizzy, I'd take longer to admire his transformation.

The five shifters pursued the monster from all angles. Bite. Claw. Retreat. They were careful to dodge the wide sweep of its arms, but James only barely dodged a blow. They were too close to it.

"Come on." I couldn't just stand around and do nothing.

I'd lost my daggers at some point while running, and I'd already discovered that my fire was useless against the Chupacabra.

"Think. Think. Think." It had to have a vulnerability.

I gripped my ribs as a fresh wave of pain racked my body. Blood seeped between my fingers, and that was when things began clicking into place.

I hadn't lost all of my daggers. Not the one that really mattered.

Screw modesty.

I ripped my shirt over my head and wiped my hand through the blood on my side to see the tattoo inked into my skin.

"Thank god." The monster's claws had just missed the tattooed blade.

Impervious to outside magic, the tattooed blade had a way of eating through the magical defenses of its victims. I just had to rip it free to use it. The dagger was intended as a last resort. Imbued with magic, it was sharper and stronger than any normal blade, but it took as much as it gave and once I ripped it free from my flesh, I'd be on a time clock. It used my own energy reserves and if it failed—though that'd yet to happen—but if it did, I'd eventually pass out. The blade would retreat to its tattooed form, and I'd be left exposed. With backup here, it was worth the risk.

I stared down at the tattoo and groaned. I hated this part.

Pressing my fingers into my flesh, I closed my eyes and reached for the blade with my senses. My fingers brushed over its hilt, and I sank them in farther until I could wrap my hand around the leather bound handle.

An inferno of pain flooded me as I pulled the blade free from my abdomen. I gritted my teeth, but it didn't keep the hiss of pain from escaping me.

It hurt. God, it hurt.

The hilt came free. Followed by the slow release of the blade.

"FUUUUUCK." The tip scored bone as it slid free.

I gasped, and my knees buckled, but I had it.

The blade sat heavy in my palm. Six inches in length, it had a wicked curve to it and a string of glyphs etched into its finish. I tightened my grip and pushed back to my feet, using every ounce of strength I had left. It'd taken maybe three minutes to pull the dagger free, but it felt like it had taken hours.

I wobbled on my feet.

A howl of pain pierced the air as one of the wolves was thrown to the side, landing with an audible crack.

He didn't get up.

Horror filled me as the wolf shifted to his human form. It was Devin, one of Declan's sentries. His body had forced him back to his human shape to recover.

Declan and James both moved with blinding speed, their claws digging into the creature with little result. Robert and the other wolf circled the monster but kept their distance. Blood dripped from evident wounds on both of them, and they were clearly tired, their breaths coming in labored huffs.

The Chupacabra reared its head and swiped out in a wide arc.

All the shifters jumped to avoid the hit, but in doing so they left a clear path between the monster and Devin's prone and naked body.

It was now or never.

Blade in hand, I ignored my own injuries and ran toward the monster. I closed the distance faster than I would have thought possible and lifted my blade with a cry of pain and fury.

"Aria! No!" James shouted.

The monster's head lifted, and blood-red eyes latched onto mine.

Come on, you ugly bastard. You can't have him.

The monster's attention returned to Devin, the easier target. It didn't matter. I was almost there.

Through my peripheral vision, I could see James running to intercept me, but he was too far.

Flames erupted along my arms, extending to the blade as I leapt into the air to land on the monster's back. I buried my free hand in fur and climbed higher until I sat astride one of its shoulders and stabbed the blade deep into its neck.

It slid in with little resistance, cutting through meat until it struck bone.

The monster bellowed in pain before reaching over its shoulder to rip me off.

I cried out, my flames faltered, but I kept my grip and used my legs for leverage as I dragged the blade across the back of its neck.

I buried the hilt, sinking part of my hand in deep through the monster's flesh, and I prayed that I struck something vital. When I hit bone again, I sank all of my weight onto the blade.

It reached for me again. A claw sinking deep into my chest above my left breast. Blood poured profusely before there was an audible snap inside of me.

I screamed.

Bone crunched and air whooshed out of my lungs. My vision clouded, and my head spun from the pain.

Come on. Hold on just a little longer.

I couldn't catch my breath. God, it'd snapped a rib and fuck, but it felt like it was stabbing my lung.

The monster swayed.

My grip slipped from my blade, and I fell back, my body weightless as I careened toward the ground.

It was okay. I did it.

Air whistled through my ears, and I knew when I landed, I was done. I tried to turn, to put myself in a position to land on my feet, but my body wasn't responding to commands. With a sick thud, I slammed into the harsh ground. The frost-covered dirt cold against my cheek.

I couldn't get up. I couldn't speak or move. My fingers twitched, but that was it. All I felt was pain. It rocked my body, stealing away my ability to think.

Seconds later, a much heavier thud vibrated the earth beneath me.

My breath shuddered in my lungs, and blood filled my mouth.

That can't be good.

"Aria. Aria! Stay with me."

Someone pulled me into a warm embrace.

My head lolled back, and exhaustion pulled at me. I just wanted to close my eyes. I needed to sleep. I needed… I wasn't sure.

I was so cold. I tried to get closer to the person holding me, but my body wouldn't respond.

"Don't close your eyes. Stay with me, just stay awake. Dammit, listen to me."

Declan was such an asshat. For once, couldn't he just leave me alone?

He shook my shoulders, and had I had the energy, I would have told him to fuck off. *It hurt.* My entire body hurt, and he wasn't making it any better. I'd killed the monster. A Chupacabra for christsakes. I'd earned a nap at the very least.

"She's lost too much blood." Leave it to James to point out the obvious.

"She'll make it. She has to." What did he care? It wasn't like Declan liked me very much.

More voices followed, but I couldn't make out their words.

Declan hoisted me in his arms. I moaned, but otherwise couldn't move. Fuck him.

A car door opened, and he placed me across the back seat before he slid in beside me. He pressed his body against mine, our faces so close that our breaths mingled together. He smelled like pine and mint.

He reached out and tucked a stray curl behind my ear. I tried to focus on him, but my vision was too hazy. My breaths came in short, wet gasps.

"I'm sorry. There's no other way."

I didn't know what he was talking about.

But I was pretty sure I was dying.

The thought should've bothered me more than it did. But I was so tired.

His hand brushed my cheek, and for a fleeting moment, I wished I could see his face. Kiss his full mouth.

Whoa. Where had that thought come from?

He smoothed my hair away and gently pressed his fingers to the sensitive skin of my neck.

"You're going to be angry. You won't understand. But… try to forgive me."

I didn't know what there was to forgive. Was he asking for forgiveness for being such an asshole all this time?

Fine. I forgave him.

I wasn't going to die with anything on my conscience.

Declan tilted my head to the side, and the heat of his breath fluttered across my skin.

I stiffened. Or tried to.

"W..What…?"

A sharp stab of pain followed a fleeting kiss. I seized in his arms, as he buried his fangs in my neck.

The fucker bit me.

And then everything went black.

Chapter Ten

I moaned and reached for my throat only to discover a dried scab beneath my fingertips on the left side.

Ow!

I opened my eyes against the harsh lights and struggled to focus on my surroundings. There was a rustle of movement to my right before a wave of worry flooded through me.

What the hell?

I turned my head, blinking several times to clear my vision. Declan approached to claim the seat beside my bed. A furrow between his brows.

"Hey."

"What happened?" I croaked. My throat was raw, and he held a small cup of water to my lips. I eyed the cup like it could bite me before huffing out a breath and taking the damn thing. I appreciated the help, but it wasn't like Declan to play nursemaid to anyone.

I took a tentative sip. The cool water soothed my dry throat.

"You lost a lot of blood. You had a punctured lung, three broken ribs, and a lacerated spleen. You're healing now, though. Just rest." He lifted a hand as if to touch me, but pulled back.

Weird.

"The Chupacabra?" I asked, sinking back into the pillows behind me.

"Dead."

I nodded. "Good." I closed my eyes for a minute, heaving a sigh of relief. "Devin and the others?"

"Devin's embarrassed, but he'll make a full recovery. The others walked away with only a few scrapes and bruises."

That was good.

The worry I'd felt only moments ago was quickly morphing into anxiety I couldn't explain. I rubbed my hands over my neck, unsure of what was happening to me.

"Are you alright?" He rested a hand over my forearm.

Warmth bloomed in my chest. His touch made me... I couldn't find the words. But the contact seemed to... *help.*

I couldn't explain it. I opened my eyes to find his emerald one's boring into mine. I felt his worry. His anticipation.

It was more than intuition. Something was wrong. Really freaking wrong.

"What's going on?" I asked.

Declan looked away. His jaw clenched.

Patience was never one of my virtues. "I feel like death warmed over. An explanation of what the hell happened would be appreciated right about now."

"I forced you into something that you didn't ask for. I'm sorry. I—"

Memories rushed back to the forefront of my mind. I ground my molars together as I leveled Declan with a death glare. "*You BIT me.*"

He flinched, but nodded.

What an insensitive asshat. I'd been dying for chrissakes!

Wait a minute. I should be dead. My rational mind knew I'd lost too much blood. My wounds had been too severe.

Accelerated healing or not, it wouldn't have been enough to save me.

But I'd killed that ugly bastard at least.

I smiled.

But then… the car. "Oh my God." I covered my face with my hands. "Am I going to turn? Fuck. Am I a… weretiger now?"

Wouldn't that just be perfect? I'd be a tiger like Declan, then he'd be my Alpha for real. He would absolutely boss me around. Even more than he already did.

Why me?

I reached my fingers into my mouth and felt around. My canines didn't feel any sharper than usual.

I stared down at my hands. Ten fingers. I pulled the blanket away from my legs and feet. Ten toes.

"Aria. Calm down."

"Dammit, Declan. Did you turn me into a shapeshifter?" I didn't feel all that different. Not like I thought I would feel if a caged animal were trapped inside of me. Would I sense my beast inside of me? Or maybe it only came out when my emotions were heightened? But if that were the case, they certainly were now.

Shit. I needed to talked to James.

"That's not how it works."

I knew that. I knew that to become a shifter there needed to be a transfer of blood. But—

"Then why the hell did you bite me?" I shoved him in the shoulder, but it had little effect. My arms were like Jell-O and I bounced against the bed.

Declan stood from his seat and paced the length of the room. His frustration palpable.

"I couldn't let you die. My tiger wouldn't let you die." He came back to the side of the bed and reached for my hand.

On instinct, I pulled away. Wary now.

I didn't want to be lying down for this conversation. I refused to be in a vulnerable position, allowing him to tower over me.

I pushed up from the bed.

My body swayed for several seconds as I fought to remain on my feet. When Declan moved to steady me, I held a hand up to halt him. I didn't need his help.

"What do you mean your tiger wouldn't let me die? What. Did. You. Do?" I punctuated each word with a slap on the bedframe.

An ache speared through my chest akin to what I'd felt when Mike died and when I'd lost my parents.

My heart plummeted into my stomach. Loss consumed me. A gut-wrenching feeling like everything I held dear was being ripped away. But these weren't my feelings.

Tears formed in the corners of my eyes, and I growled in frustration. Dammit, I would not cry. I didn't have anything to be upset over. No one had died. No one was seriously hurt. What the hell was wrong with me?

I was terrified that I was about to lose the most precious thing in the world to me. Where was that coming from?

"Declan—what the hell did you do?"

His eyes were downcast. His expression full of remorse. It broke something inside of me to see him like this.

"You were dying."

"But I'm here, and I'm fine now."

He was shaking his head. "You weren't going to make it if I didn't intervene. Your pulse was already fading. If I'd hesitated for even a minute, it would have been too late." He paused before steeling himself to face me.

His eyes met mine. Filled with flecks of gold, I could see the beast lurking within their depths. "When a shifter takes a mate—"

My breath caught. My heart pounded in my chest. "Mate..." I whispered.

No. No. No.

"—if the mating is true, a bond forms. This bond connects two people. It allows them to share strength in times of struggle. To lean on one another for both emotional and physical support."

I waited for him to continue. Something inside of me knew he wasn't finished.

"When an Alpha takes a mate, he has the strength of the entire Pack behind him. If either he or his mate are injured, they can pull strength from the Pack—to heal—to survive."

My breathing hitched.

"You needed that strength, Aria." He ran a shaky hand through his short, white-blond hair. "It shouldn't have worked. The bond doesn't always form. It can take months, years even, and sometimes it never forms at all. But with you, it was instant. Aria, I felt you." He placed his right hand on his chest right over his heart. "I felt you right here. Right away. You're my mate."

Sonovabitch.

"You mate-claimed me?" I was going to kill him.

"I didn't have a choice."

Like hell he hadn't. But before I could tell him so, the door to the room swung wide and James stepped in. "Hey, you're—"

"You let him mate-claim me?!" I demanded, cutting him off. "What the hell were you thinking?" I threw one of my boots at him.

James easily dodged it before looking away, standing by the door awkwardly.

"What the hell, James?"

"You were dying, Ari!" He faced me, his grey eyes pleading with me to understand.

"No. Don't you 'Ari' me. I'm freaking mate-bonded to him." I pointed at Declan, ignoring his flinch at my tone. "How could you let him do this to me?"

A flash of grief washed over James's face before his expression went blank. He was shutting me out.

He swallowed hard. "Declan did what was necessary to save your life. The two of you formed a mate bond. You should be happy. Not everyone gets that in life."

I scoffed. "Are you kidding me?"

I turned to Declan, anger pulsing in my veins. "Fix this."

"What do you want me to do?" he asked, clearly deflated.

"Take it back."

He shook his head. "I can't do that."

There had to be a way. There had to be something, anything, that could be done to make all of this go away.

Fire rushed through my veins. It seeped through my pores, and thin wisps of flame danced along my skin.

I searched by the foot of the bed, retrieving my other boot and haphazardly shoving my foot into it before looking around for my daggers. I lifted the hem of my shirt, happy to see my tattooed blade whole and on my flesh. Shoving the shirt back down, I scanned the bed and night stands for my twin blades.

Bingo. On the bedside table. I didn't bother contemplating who'd found them for me after the fight. I grabbed my sheath and strapped it around my thigh before turning around and storming over to James.

I glared at him as I bent down to take back my other boot.

"You're on fire," he said.

"Do you really think being on fire is what I'm worried about right now?"

He pressed his lips into a thin line.

"I have to get out of here." I moved to shove past him.

"You can't leave." Declan said behind me.

I whirled on him so fast I gave myself whiplash. "You do not own me. I am not yours. And I do not take orders from you. I don't care that you said you mate-claimed me. I'm going to fix this. With or without your help."

I had no idea how I was going to do that exactly, but eh, semantics. One way or another, I would reverse whatever he had done to me.

"There isn't anything to fix, Aria. This isn't a bad thing. The bond already formed. This is real. It's permanent."

I sneered at him. "Maybe to you it is, but I didn't ask for this. I don't want any part in it."

"Hey, calm down." James reached for me, and I jerked away.

Taking two more steps toward the door, I found myself blocked by a solid wall of muscle. How the hell had he gotten there so fast?

Declan's eyes were hard as ice. "I can't let you leave like this. You need to calm down."

Calm down? Was he kidding? How the hell was I supposed to calm down? I saw red when I realized he was going to try to force me to stay. My fire grew without conscious thought, and within seconds, my arms were engulfed in orange flames.

"Get out of my way," I gritted the words out between clenched teeth.

He didn't move. His face was an expressionless mask, but whatever bond had formed between us allowed me to feel the emotions swirling inside of him, and he was wary. Good.

He wouldn't hurt me, and when I was like this, he couldn't reasonably stop me either. Seconds ticked by, and my patience thinned.

I took another step forward.

He didn't move.

I weighed my options and finally decided to hell with it all. I walked right into him, my hands pushing against his chest as I allowed the flames to lick his flesh in my attempt to shove past him.

He hissed, but he still didn't move.

I shoved his chest harder.

The smell of burned flesh permeated the room. The center of

his thermal shirt burned away, and once-smooth skin blistered beneath my hands.

But the stubborn jerk remained immobile. His face granite and his mouth pressed into a tight, thin line. A muscle ticked in his jaw.

I couldn't take it anymore. I jerked away. "Let me go." My voice shook, and I cringed at the plea in my voice.

Declan didn't say anything, but a silent communication passed between him and James.

James nodded, and Declan gave me one last long, searching look, and then turned and left the room.

I folded my still flaming arms across my chest and counted to ten as I tried to rein in my fire. James stood by in silence, waiting patiently.

When I hit ten, nothing happened. The flames still burned, so I tried again. On the fourth round, my flames retreated.

"Ari—"

"James, just… don't."

I needed air. I needed to get away from everything that was Pack. And that included James. He was supposed to be my best friend, but right now, I didn't know what he was. How could he let Declan do this to me?

"Look, I know this is a lot to take in."

I snorted. "You think?"

"Would you just talk to me and cut the bullshit?" His eyes were so sincere, so genuine, that I found myself nodding without even realizing it.

He smiled and led me over to the bed. He took a seat beside me, and when I went to cross my arms, he pulled my hand away, clasping it in his as we sat beside one another.

He didn't say anything at first. He just stared at the blank stone wall in front of us.

"A mate bond doesn't happen often. It's a sign of finding your one true match. Your soul mate."

Declan wasn't my soul mate. He couldn't be. I could barely stand the guy. "How was I claimed to begin with? I remember him biting me"—my hand brushed my neck—"but that's all I remember."

"There's a serum that releases when a shifter bites their mate. Only your beast knows when the time is right. And his tiger decided you were its mate, so it claimed you."

"Why did you let him do this to me?" I asked, my voice barely audible to my own ears. "I trusted you." I looked up at James's stricken expression.

With his free hand, he covered his face, taking a deep breath before turning to look at me.

I knew I shouldn't blame him. But I was hurt and angry. He'd been there. Why hadn't he done something—anything—to stop him?

"Ari, I thought you were going to die. We all did."

"Then you should have let me die."

"Don't say that. Don't ever fucking say that. I could never let you die, not if there was another way." He released my hand and tugged at the strands of his hair. "Fuck."

"You can't let me die, but you can let me be mate-claimed against my will? How is that any better?"

"Then you being dead? Aria, what the hell are you even thinking? Of course, being mate-claimed is better than death."

Not to me, it wasn't. This wasn't like dating or being married. This was an ownership. It wouldn't have been so bad if it'd been with someone else. Someone who I was on equal footing with. But I'd been claimed by the Alpha of all Alphas in our region.

"I need to get out of here." I stood up.

"Where are you going to go?" he asked.

"I don't know, but I can't stay here. Not like this."

He reached out and gave my hand a squeeze. "I get that you

need some time and some space. Declan gets it, too." He stopped me before I could interrupt him. "He gets it. Give the guy some credit. You should know that you're his everything now. He would never hurt you. And your happiness is his number one priority."

I didn't entirely believe him. While the bond made me almost certain that he'd never intentionally hurt me physically, it didn't reassure me that he wouldn't crush me another way. I'd had my spirit crushed enough in the past. And Declan was possessive and domineering. I couldn't let him bulldoze over me.

"I would have done it in his place if it would have been enough. If I'd had enough strength to save you." James's words were whispered beneath his breath, but he may as well have shouted them in the quiet room for how hard they hit me.

My eyes misted at his confession and I wrapped my arms around him in a tight embrace, burying my face in his chest.

I knew he would have, and I loved him for it, but I wasn't the girl for him. I wasn't happy Declan had claimed me, but I was glad it hadn't been James. He deserved better than me.

"I know," I said before pulling away and leaving my room and the Compound behind me.

Chapter Eleven

An hour after leaving the Compound, my phone went off. I ignored the first three calls—recognizing the number as Declan's—before turning the phone off entirely.

What ever happened to giving me some space?

I'd had to leave on foot since my car was still at Mr. Ortiz's, and with every mile I traveled farther away from the Compound, a small part of me died a little inside. It was like my body knew I was leaving him, and it rejected the idea. This bond was serious business, and I was not at all happy about it.

There had to be a way to undo it. I racked my brain for anything that could get me out of this. And came up with zilch.

Shifters were secretive. I wasn't holding my breath that anyone outside a Pack would know of a way to get out of the mate bond. Assuming it were even possible. And no Pack member was going to go against Declan. Not even James. So that let me with few options.

But maybe I was wrong. Maybe another paranormal would have an idea. Melody Leis was my friend, and I knew she'd be willing to help me if she could. She was a harpy, and while not privy to shifter operations, she knew more about all things paranormal than I did.

It was worth a try.

I powered up my cell phone again, deleted my missed calls log, and dialed her number. Her ring back tone sang in my ear. A No Doubt song from before my time. "Holla back, girl! What's up?" she said enthusiastically.

"Holla what?"

"Don't judge. I'm trying something new."

I sighed. She was always trying something new, and I had a feeling this was yet another thing having to do with our neighbor Ryan. I really wished she'd embrace who she was, as she was, without all this new crap to get his attention.

"Mel, I need some help." And with that one statement, she turned all business.

"Who do I need to kill?" Her tone was entirely serious.

I had to laugh. Melody was the friend you called when there was a dead body in your living room that needed taking care of. She was the ride or die type. And rather than freaking out and asking what the hell happened, she'd ask you where you kept your shovels and help you start digging.

Hell, she probably wouldn't even ask you that much—she'd find the damn things herself. When she called you friend, there was nothing she wouldn't do for you.

"No one. Not yet, at least. I just—" There was no sugarcoating this and if I wanted help, I needed to be honest. Full transparency here. "I've been mate-bonded to the Alpha of the Pacific Northwest Pack."

The line went silent.

"Mel?" Had she hung up on me? I looked down at my phone screen. Nope. Still connected.

"You're fucking with me, right?"

"God, I wish I was." Wasn't that the understatement of the

century? I rubbed at my forehead. If Mel didn't have any ideas, I'd be up a creek without a paddle.

"Where are you? I'm grabbing my bag and leaving right now."

Oh, thank God.

I surveyed my surroundings. I'd walked several miles after leaving the Compound before hailing a cab to drop me as close to town as the twenty in my pocket could get me.

"I'm on Argonne, nearing Millwood. Can you meet me at the Rocket Bakery?"

"Done. See you in ten." With that she hung up, and I released a huge sigh of relief. Melody was on her way. I'd explain the situation—well, as best I could—and together we'd hash out a plan to get rid of the bond. Easy-peasy, right?

I shoved my phone in my pocket and continued to walk at a brisk pace, getting closer to the Millwood area of Spokane.

I shook my head, wishing I had my Civic. I'd need to come up with a way to get it back without asking Declan or James for a lift. Maybe Mel could help me out after we spoke.

The roads were filled with traffic that was at a standstill. Some idiot had turned down Argonne the wrong way, not realizing it was a one-way road. I'd missed the wreck, but not the aftermath. The absence of any fire trucks or ambulance was nothing new. We'd yet to recover some of the most basic forms of community help since the Awakening. Though not paying taxes was nice.

When paranormals decided to come out of hiding, our government waged a war they just couldn't win. That was the problem with human society. As a species, we were driven by fear, and more than anything, humans feared the unknown.

Our president at the time had funneled all financial resources into our military. He'd pulled funds from each state, bankrupting both state and federal governments in an attempt to kill the monsters coming out of the shadows.

Military forces failed. They'd been ill equipped to fight an enemy they knew nothing about. A handful of months later, a thin agreement was made for the sake of all species involved, and all parties stepped back in an attempt at peace. We'd all suffered casualties.

Shortly thereafter our democracy fell. Six years later, we'd pieced ourselves back together, but things would never be the same. Most cities had a shaky system in place to govern themselves. But without a statewide governing body, taxes, and state programs, we'd yet to put vital systems like emergency responders into place.

The closest thing we had to a police system in Washington was the HPED. They were currently on the scene of the traffic jam, but didn't appear to be doing much. One vehicle—a lifted Ford truck—was off to the side of the road with little more than a scratch. In the middle of the street rested a small white car. I could barely tell that it had been a car to begin with. It looked more like a crushed tin can on wheels. Well, two wheels to be exact. The other two were farther down the road, having come off during the collision.

I needed to get past them in order to get to the coffee shop, and as I approached, a woman began wildly yelling at the HPED men. She waved her arms frantically in the air as she gave her story, and I fought an eye roll as I ducked my head and walked past, trying to look unassuming.

I slipped through two buildings and made my way to the front entrance of the Rocket Bakery Coffee House. The door chimed as I walked in.

"What the hell took you so long?" Mel practically steamrolled me as she pulled me into her embrace.

This was weird. We'd never hugged before.

My arms stayed stiff at my sides, and when Melody pulled away, a frown marred her near-perfect features. Her raven-colored hair fell in waves around her shoulders, and she sported another flashy schoolgirl outfit—a red, plaid, mini skirt and a black, button-up top that left her cleavage on full display. Paired with black fishnet stockings and ballet flats, she looked all sorts of wrong.

"I think a better question is what the hell are you wearing?" I raised an eyebrow.

She frowned. "Ignore the outfit and just come sit down. You've had me worried sick."

"I didn't know harpies worried. And seriously, you've got a lot of explaining to do. You look like a schoolgirl stripper recently released from prison."

Melody stuck her tongue out at me.

"Why are you wearing this crap?"

"That idiot keeps bringing home these schoolgirl wannabes. I swear I don't know why I even bother. I look ridiculous."

"Not ridiculous at all," I chimed in. "But maybe don't be so obvious." She glared at me when I smothered a laugh.

"If it was so obvious, you'd think he'd have noticed by now." She huffed. Melody had a crush on Ryan Cavanagh—our very human neighbor. He lived in the same apartment building, and as a musician, he often came home with groupies and for whatever reason, Mel felt the need to compete with the skanks.

"Give him time. He'll figure it out." At least I hoped he did. Ryan was a good guy, but he could be a little dense.

Melody huffed out another breath, and I hid my smile before she wiped it off my face with her next words.

"So, how did you end up bonded to the Alpha?"

I sighed heavily and ran my hands through my hair. I may as well start at the beginning. "Mike left me Sanborn Place," I told her. "I feel like he saw more in me than I ever did, and with him gone, I wanted to do things right so I went straight to work." she nodded.

"I called old clients to let them know Sanborn Place was still in business." Looking back, maybe I shouldn't have rushed into it so quickly. Maybe then I wouldn't be in this mess. "I got my first gig the other day. A farmer hired me to find some creature eating his goats."

"How does a gig wind up with you mate-bonded?"

"I'm getting to that part and by the way, the gig involved a Chupacabra."

Her eyes widened. "You're kidding?"

I shook my head. "No, it was the real deal. The bastard was damn near impossible to kill, so I called for backup. James came to the rescue with a carful of shifters. Declan was with him. Things got hairy, and I ended up half dead by the time the Chupacabra finally went down."

"Of course, you did. I can't believe you went up against one of them. They're freaking legends in Mexico. Almost impossible to kill."

"Thanks for the memo," I said sardonically.

"So, the Alpha mate-claimed you to save your life?" she guessed.

I nodded.

"Makes sense."

"How the hell does any of that make sense to you?" I didn't want her to understand why he'd done it. I wanted her to be angry along with me at the sheer audacity of him claiming me without my permission.

Mel shrugged her shoulders. "Well, I'd hate to find out you were dead, so I guess this is the lesser of two evils."

I lowered my head to the table. The surface was cool against my forehead. "Why is everyone on his side?" I whined. "I don't want to be claimed. I want a way out of this." I raised my head to peer up at her and rested my chin in my hands.

Mel's eyes softened. It wasn't often I was on the receiving end of sympathy, and it made me uncomfortable. "There isn't anything you can do," she said, shaking her head. "I'll do some digging just in case. I have some friends who may have an idea, but as far as I know, the only way to break a mate bond is through death and even then…" She trailed off, shrugging her shoulders.

"And even then…?"

She turned away, her eyes scanning the room for a moment. "Did the two of you form a bond?"

I nodded. "He says we did. I can feel him inside of me. His emotions. It's creepy as hell."

"Shifters mate for life. Their beasts don't take that bond lightly. When one dies, their mate usually follows shortly after. The bond is that strong."

Great. Just great. Not only was I bonded, my life was also tied to his. Could this get any worse?

Chapter Twelve

Mel had been a dead end, but it had helped to vent. Sometimes you just needed a person to validate your feelings, and she'd done that for me.

She dropped me off downtown after we finished our coffee and offered to stick around, but really, I just wanted to be alone. I walked around for a bit before making my way back to my apartment. I had no desire to go back to the Compound.

The day was nearing its end, the sun having set close to an hour ago. The streets were silent but for the whistling wind. I hunched my shoulders against the cold and pulled the lapels of my leather jacket tighter. I walked a few blocks before taking a left on 2nd Avenue. I'd circle around Sanborn Place—making sure everything was locked up tight—and then head home.

A flash of red in my peripheral vision snagged my attention, and I turned to watch a familiar figure slip from a nearby alley to run across the street. Dressed in black leggings and a light-grey sweater, there was no missing Irina's waist-length red hair.

Before I could think, I jogged across the street after her.

Her steps were silent, her attention focused on where she was going instead of on who may be following her, and I kept pace without being noticed.

I followed her down several streets, ducking behind dumpsters and into alcoves to avoid being seen. After four blocks, she stopped and scanned the vacant street.

I held my breath and waited for her to spot me.

She didn't, and after one last cursory look behind her, she climbed up a set of brick steps leading into a two-story townhouse. When the door closed behind her, I jogged forward for a closer look.

Inarus claimed she'd been the one behind Daniel's death. If that were true, then we had a score to settle.

There was little cover at the front of the townhouse, so I went around to the side and hoped that the shadows would be enough to hide me. Sleet and slush crunched beneath my boots as I followed the perimeter until I came to a main floor window and peered inside.

Sheer draperies blocked most of my view, but I could make out a lone figure with red hair. She moved into an adjoining room, and I crept farther around the outside until I came to another window, this one without coverings.

Irina entered the room and took a seat with her back to the window. I couldn't see her face, but a man now stood to her right, facing her. He waved his hands through the air as he spoke.

I wished I could hear what they were talking about. Whatever it was, he was enthusiastic in his pursuit to share his words with a seemingly uninterested Irina.

She made no movements. No gestures that even hinted she was paying attention.

I watched in silence, crouched low in my efforts to remain unseen. The wind whipped my hair in my face, and the cool temperatures made my breath fog up the glass in front of me. I had to fight the urge to wipe at it.

A cramp formed in my right leg as the minutes ticked by.

Snow flurried from the skies, and I wished I had a coat with a hood on it instead of my leather jacket. Moisture seeped through the soles of my boots as snow slipped through the collar of my jacket to hit bare skin. Shifting my stance, I tried to get rid of the cramp when my boot slipped on the pavement. It sent me crashing toward the ground in an ungraceful heap.

I let out a tiny squeak and barely caught myself with my hands before face-planting on the pavement. Wet gravel cut into my palms.

That was close.

I bit my tongue to keep from cursing, but realized my mistake too late as the metallic tang of blood filled my mouth.

Shit. How could I be so stupid?

Vampires were like bloodhounds. Even a drop of blood called to them, and I wasn't that far away from one, possibly two. If my fall hadn't alerted them to my presence, the scent of my blood would.

Today really wasn't my day.

As expected, the sound of the front door opening echoed through the dark streets.

I scurried to stand and make a quick getaway, but I wasn't quick enough. I'd barely taken three steps when someone yanked me back by my braid.

Urgh, I really needed to reconsider cutting my hair. Vanity was so not worth this.

"Who do we have here?" a malicious voice whispered in my ear. The man's grip was firm as he jerked my head farther back.

I pulled a blade from my sheath and palmed the dagger. "Your worst nightmare." It wasn't the most original line, but it did the job.

Ignoring the sting of my hair being pulled from my scalp. I twisted around and plunged the blade deep into my assailant's chest.

He released me immediately and stared down at the dagger

imbedded in his chest as he staggered back. It wasn't lethal, but it should keep him busy for a little while.

Now that we were face to face, I could see that he wasn't a vampire. But the blackened blood that oozed from the wound meant he was a vampire's blood servant. His life bound to his master and his humanity already stripped. He stumbled back and slumped against the ground.

Down for the count.

I scanned the area for Irina. She was retreating in the opposite direction with her cloak pulled up to cover her features.

"Coward," I snarled angrily. I took two steps in her direction. "I know who you are. And I'm sure Rebecka will be curious to know why one of her inner circle is conducting secret meetings behind her back."

Her steps faltered, but she didn't turn to face me.

"I know you were behind Daniel's death. And I know that you're working to ruin the truce between the Pack and the Coven."

She turned. Slowly. Her eyes a malicious red as they honed in on me.

"You don't know what you're talking about," she spat. Her lips pulled back, exposing her fangs.

Guess I'd struck a chord. "Oh, I do, and I'm sure when I tell Rebecka all about it, she'll be so disappointed with you." I tsked. "I wonder what she'll do to you."

Irina's eyes focused on the blood servant slumped behind me. "Kill her."

Why did everyone always want to kill me?

The blood servant struggled to rise to his feet. "Yes, Mistress."

I rolled my eyes. "Really? He's hardly a challenge."

He ripped the dagger from his chest.

"I wouldn't do that if I were you."

He ignored me and made a failed attempt to stab me with my

own blade. I swatted him away like the bug he was. Without medical attention, and soon, he would be dead.

I glanced over my shoulder but couldn't see Irina any longer. Dammit. I didn't have time for this.

I called my fire. Flames erupted over my body, and I sent a concentrated blaze toward my attacker.

He didn't even have time to react.

A howl of pain pierced the night as he fell back, the flames quickly engulfing him. He rolled across the pavement, screaming out for Irina to help him, but she was nowhere in sight.

"She doesn't care," I told him. And neither did I.

A minute ticked by before he stopped moving.

I couldn't leave a burning corpse on the side of the road where just anyone could find it, so I waited. His screams died down and before long, a black corpse rested at my feet, the skin breaking off in large flaking pieces before turning to ash that melted into the snow.

With the flames finished, I retrieved my dagger and ran in the direction she'd gone.

An arm shot out from the alley, and I narrowly missed her blow.

Cool calculation met my gaze as Irina stepped out of the shadows.

"Why did you do it?" I asked. "Why'd you kill the boy?"

Her lip curled. "Why are you asking me? You seem to know so much already." She balled her hands into fists at her sides. And I waited for the strike I knew would come.

I wanted her to admit what she'd done and why before I killed her. I needed to know without a shadow of a doubt that she'd been the culprit, because after I took her down, I'd have hell to pay with the Coven.

It'd all be worth it, though.

"Did you enjoy the visit from my associate the other day?" she sneered at me.

"That was your doing?" After my conversation with Inarus, I'd suspected Irina had been responsible for the rogue that attacked me outside Sanborn Place. She was old, but I hadn't thought her old enough to turn someone.

Then again, how would I know?

"Yes, my first. He was lovely, wasn't he?"

"You threw him away." I called my fire to me and let it boil just beneath my skin. My right hand turned orange and Irina's gaze didn't miss it, but she pretended like it wasn't anything to worry about.

She waved her hand like I was of little consequence.

"I thought your kind valued its young more than that?"

"I have little use for a child. He had a purpose, and he failed. There is not much more to it." She really was a cold-hearted bitch.

"Why do all of this? You're in the Coven's inner circle. You have power and status. Why try to destroy the treaty between the Pack and the Coven? Why try to kill me?"

"Stupid girl. The Coven and the Pack are mortal enemies. There never should have been a treaty. Shifters are nothing more than vicious beasts that need to be collared. Rebecka made an alliance with those savages, and for what? The greater good? For who? Certainly not for our own kind. No, she was foolish, and I am simply correcting her mistake."

"Behind her back. Do you really think you'll get away with it?" She had to know Rebecka would find out, eventually.

"When the shifters are crushed, the Coven will stand beside me, and Rebecka's opinions will no longer matter. We need a strong leader, not one who believes in peace with our enemy."

"That won't ever happen. The Pack and Rebecka are well aware that someone is working to incite a war between them. Both sides are taking precautions. Your plan won't work."

"Oh, it will. You just won't live long enough to see it." I raised my glowing hand to strike her but at her final word, I felt a crushing weight slam into my skull, knocking me to the side and onto the pavement.

"I hit her, Mistress, I hit her!" a voice said giddily behind me.

Fuck, that hurt. Where the hell had he come from?

"Well, hit her again and make sure she doesn't get up."

Footsteps retreated. I tried to call my fire, but my head was swimming. A booted foot came within my view, and the shadow of a man cast over me. Another blood servant? How many of the bastards did she have?

"Sorry, miss. Must do what Mistress says."

I tried to focus on the man before me and struggled into a sitting position. I needed my fire, but I was seeing stars. I tried anyway. Flames flickered on the tips of my fingers but extinguished in less than a second.

Come on, Aria. Focus.

I pushed harder, watching in horror as he moved to strike again. I raised my hands above my head.

Burn, you bastard. Burn.

It wasn't working.

A crash sounded, and I watched through hazy vision as the servant's body slammed into the wall of a house, whatever object he'd used to hit me falling from his fingers as unconsciousness stole him.

"Aria, are you okay?" Inarus's voice met my ears, and for once I was happy to hear it. Relief swept through me before I realized Irina was probably long gone by now.

"Irina… getting… away," I coughed out.

"I know. Don't worry about that. We need to get you somewhere safe." He lifted me in his arms, and before I could take my next breath, ported us from the street into a sterile-looking room with a row of hospital beds lining the wall and a fully stocked medicine cupboard to my right. That was all I saw before the dizziness in my head roared and unconsciousness took me under.

Chapter Thirteen

You'd think I'd be used to waking up in strange places with how often I passed out. But I wasn't. As my eyes adjusted to the light in the room, it didn't take long to realize Inarus was with me and the two of us were not alone.

Well, shit.

"How are you feeling?" he asked.

I scrubbed a hand over my face. "Like I just got hit in the head with a sledgehammer." I groaned and tried to sit up.

"Actually, it was a two-by-four, but close enough."

Raising a brow, I glowered at him. Not funny.

I rubbed the ache at the back of my skull, my hand coming away with dried flecks of blood. Nothing fresh, though, and I didn't feel any stitches, so that was a good sign. Things could have been worse. The splitting headache was certainly enough.

"I'm so glad you're alright, sweetheart" a strange, but familiar, voice said.

My gaze landed on my mother, and I froze. Dressed in a navy pantsuit with a peach-colored top, she looked like an influential businesswoman. Her hair was expertly pulled back, not a strand out of place, and her makeup flawlessly applied.

She didn't look like my mother. The mother who used to brush my hair before bed. Whose hands were always caked in flour. No. The two women couldn't be more opposite. There was no warmth in this woman's eyes. She was little more than a stranger to me, but she was staring down at me with a wide-mouthed smile and she'd called me sweetheart.

What the hell?

"Um… hi," was all I was able to muster.

I looked at Inarus for help, and all I got was a shrug of his shoulders. Perfect. Real helpful.

My mother—correction. Viola—came closer and sat on the edge of the bed. She reached out and grasped my hand in hers, her touch cold and uncomfortable. I fought the urge to pull away, morbidly curious more than anything to see where this would go.

The little girl inside of me wanted to leap into her arms, but the woman in me knew better. She wasn't the mother I'd grown up with. Not by a long shot. And whatever childish dreams I may have clung on to vanished the moment I realized she was alive and well.

I pulled my hand from hers and folded my arms against my chest, ignoring the look of hurt that crossed her features. I wasn't buying it. God, had she always been like this? Practiced and perfect with no real warmth or substance to her?

"Can we get you anything? Food? Something to drink?"

I shook my head, doing my best to ignore the sickening sensation of the room spinning. Note to self, don't shake your head after you get hit with a two by four.

What I wanted were answers. But I wasn't sure that either of us was ready for that conversation quite yet.

"Very well. Rest. We'll talk more tomorrow when you've recovered. We have so much to catch up on."

We did. Yay me. I wondered if she could feel my sarcasm

because with that one statement, she left. It was the most awkward non-conversation I'd ever had with anyone in my life.

When the door clicked behind her, and Inarus and I were alone, I turned on him. "What the hell were you thinking, bringing me here?"

"I was thinking you needed medical attention, and this was the best option. The only option."

I frowned. He was probably right, but I still didn't like it. I swung my legs over the side of the bed. Determined to get the hell out of there.

My vision swam for several seconds, and I clutched my head with one hand, the other clinging to the wall until the world righted itself.

"Whoa, take it easy."

"I need to get out of here." I knew myself pretty well, and I was not emotionally capable of dealing with this situation. Not today. Not tomorrow. Hell, not next week.

"No, you need to rest." He placed a hand on my shoulder and gently nudged me back to the bed.

I glared at him. "You brought me to what—my mother's freaking headquarters? Do you have any idea how weird that is?" And how fucked up?

"Yes, I do. And I'm sorry about that, but you'd end up coming face to face with her, eventually."

Didn't mean it had to be now. I was an expert at avoiding my problems, and my mother was one big ole problem that I was ready and eager to avoid.

"It wasn't your place." I took measured breaths. My head continued spinning, and if I had any hope of leaving, I would need to pull myself together so I could walk out on my own two feet. I doubted Inarus would be much help.

He shrugged his shoulders, unfazed.

Jerk.

"Look, why don't you stick around for a while? You've already gotten past the whole awkward meeting with your long-lost mother. It can't get any worse, and besides, what do you have to lose?"

My sanity, for one. That was something I was very likely to lose if I stuck around. How was I supposed to deal with something like this?

My phone buzzed in my jeans, and I quickly dug it out. Declan's name flashed across the screen, and without any thought, I sent the call to voicemail. There was only so much a girl could handle.

I only then realized I had eleven missed calls from him in the last twenty minutes. Oops.

I pulled up my voicemail and listened to his most recent message.

"Aria, what happened? I know you were hurt. I felt it. Just... call me back." His voice was strained.

I hadn't realized how deep the bond went. I'd hoped that with distance, it would lessen. When we were in the same room, I'd felt his emotions like they were my own, but now... I rubbed at my chest. It was less. Ignorable. Wait, was that even a word?

I considered deleting the messages and turning my phone off, but I had a feeling all it would do was put him on a manhunt. I had no desire to be his quarry, so instead I did the responsible thing. I sent him a text.

I'm fine. It was nothing. Please give me some space.

See, real mature. After that, I powered my phone down and shoved it back in my pocket. Okay, I was a coward, but at least I'd adulted enough and told him I was okay. It didn't mean I was ready for a conversation, though.

See, expert at avoiding my problems.

I turned back to Inarus and debated the pros and cons to

sticking around. If I left now, what would she think? Would she even care?

I wanted her to care. And God, I hated that. Hated that the little girl inside of me wanted, no needed, her mom. Urgh.

I wasn't ready to go back to the Compound—not yet.

Maybe this could be a good thing. Irina was still on the loose. I had her to deal with, but I now knew she was responsible for Daniel's death. I also knew she'd been working with the HAC in some capacity. Maybe if I stuck around, I'd be able to dig up more. See how deep things really went and just how dirty my own mother's hands were.

That was what I'd do. I'd stay and do a little recon. Snoop around. See what I could uncover.

I considered calling Rebecka. It didn't sit right with me, knowing Irina was out there doing God only knew what, but I also knew Rebecka would be quick to act—assuming she even believed me—and I still had questions that needed answering.

"Fine, I'll stay. But not for long. This is entirely temporary." I was still pissed at him, but that was yet another bucket of worms I didn't want to open.

He seemed satisfied with the response, and this time when I swung my legs over, he didn't stop me. "That doesn't mean I'm just going to lie in bed all day, though. Why don't you show me around or something?" Time for that recon.

Inarus perked up at the idea and took me on a tour of the facility. It was strange walking side by side with him. I had to remind myself he was the enemy. He was so animated as we walked around, telling me all about the facility, the training rooms, the state-of-the-art weapons cache they housed. I might have perked up a bit when he showed me a wall covered with medieval swords and daggers. I was a sucker for blades, but I hid my excitement and gave them only a cursory inspection before we moved on.

He'd had plans to bring me in. To bring me here to this

facility, and he'd never once told me about. At no point did he sit me down and have a conversation. But looking back, I realized I didn't know if he would have done so forcefully. Questions filled my head. What if he was planning to tell me? What if he was just working up the nerve to break the ice?

I resisted the urge to shake my head. No. Don't let good looks and him saving your life twice now fool you, Aria. He wanted war between the Coven and the shifter Pack, too. He'd killed Emma and whoever the vampire was that we'd found dead beside her. He wasn't one of the good guys, no matter how good his act.

The reminder did little to ease the glimmer of hope unfurling inside of me the longer we were together. I wanted to believe he'd been brainwashed by all of this and just needed someone to show him the error of his ways. I didn't want him to be irredeemable.

A girl could hope, right?

Inarus took me to several common areas, a recreational room, eating quarters, and what appeared to be an indoor park. The green space, as he called it, was breathtaking. Lush grasses and moss coated the ground along with tulips, daisies, and other wildflowers. I paused briefly by the daffodils, fingering the bright yellow petals.

Large willows were among the trees scattered throughout, and from somewhere in the distance, I heard running water, the distinct gurgle of a stream.

The air was mildly humid, and despite knowing we were in the thick of winter here in Spokane, the room felt like summer. I could spend hours just sitting on one of the large boulders, taking in the scenery and reading a good book.

This was a great space to meditate in.

"How is this even possible?" I asked as Inarus led me farther in. I peeled my leather jacket off and hung it over one arm, hiding my wince as my neck and shoulder throbbed in protest.

"The green space belongs to our phytokinetics. They're psykers like you and me. They manipulate plants."

I leaned down to touch a red fern, the leaves soft between my fingertips. "This is surreal."

"It's pretty amazing when you first experience it. But you get used to it. Psykers can do many amazing things. You haven't had the chance to meet others like you." He grinned, his eyes lighting up with mischief. "I'm glad I was your first."

I snorted.

"Will I be meeting any of them?" I asked, curious about these phytokinetics. It reminded me of the story The Secret Garden. My father used to read it to me when I little. The green space felt otherworldly, like I'd just passed through the gates into a secret garden world. There was something almost nostalgic about it.

"Follow me. I can see Kieran from here."

I allowed Inarus to lead me down a winding path to a small stream feeding into a pond.

"How did this get here?" I asked, unable to stop the question from spilling out of my mouth.

Another smile. "Hydrokinetics."

I nodded. It made sense. They had phytokinetics to maintain plant life and hydrokinetics to manipulate the water. It was all so fascinating.

We crossed a small wooden bridge and approached a man doing a perfectly executed crane pose. There were no tremors in his arms, no sign of discomfort from the exercise. His body moved fluidly from the crane pose to a supported headstand.

I still struggled with the tree pose, and that was beginner yoga. This—this had to have taken years of practice.

I studied him as we neared. He wore a sleeveless linen shirt and pants in an aqua color, bright against the greenery surrounding him.

A thin sheen of sweat coated his exposed arms, and his russet-colored hair was plastered to his pale skin. His movements appeared effortless, though I knew from experience that yoga only looked to be easy. In truth, it was difficult and took a significant amount of dedication and patience. Probably why I was so bad at it.

He lowered his legs with slow measured movements, then pushed from the earthen floor to stand.

My gaze shifted, and I found myself swimming in twin orbs of rich moss. His eyes changed color the longer I looked into them. Altering between shades of green and rich browns as though they couldn't decide what color they wanted to be.

A wide smile spread across his face.

I realized I'd been staring and looked away, heat climbing up my face.

"You must be Aria." He extended his hand.

I nodded mutely, immediately regretting the movement, and shook his hand instead.

"I'm Kieran, it's nice to meet you."

How did he know my name? Maybe Inarus mentioned me at some point?

Inarus placed his arm around my shoulders in what I'm sure he hoped was a casual move, but I saw it for what it was. He was claiming me in front of Kieran. I'd been claimed once already without my consent, and Inarus's attempt was just as unacceptable.

I shrugged out from under his arm and took a step towards a nearby tree, not missing the smirk on Kieran's face for the look of annoyance on Inarus's.

"Are you the one responsible for all of this?" I asked, indicating the tree and everything else around.

"Not entirely, but I'm one of three who work to maintain it."

"It's amazing. It reminds me of the Hoh Rainforest in western Washington." The tree canopy was thick and flourishing, making it easy to forget we were inside of an actual building.

"Thank you." He inclined his head, but said nothing further.

"Kieran is a man of few words. We'll let you return to your mediation."

I smiled at him as Inarus led me farther into the green space.

"There are others here that you can meet, too. If you'd like."

My gaze met his, and in it, I saw so much hope. I almost felt bad knowing it didn't matter how many people I met or how many amazing spaces he showed me. This was cool, sure. But I knew who I was and what I stood for.

I didn't belong here.

Lately, I felt like I didn't belong anywhere.

"I'd like that," I said, ignoring the pang of guilt in my chest.

Wandering the halls of the HAC was more intriguing than I'd expected. Our next stop was an atrium unlike anything I'd seen before.

The expansive glass ceiling filled the room with sunlight, but what was most impressive were the metal objects lining the floor. Spheres in varying sizes were scattered throughout the room. Some on concrete surfaces no larger than grapes, others standing taller than Inarus.

"Any idea what this room is?" He gave me a sly smile.

"I'm going to take a wild guess and say this is where TKs like yourself spend their time."

He nodded and pulled out the three metal spheres he carried in his pocket. Seconds after he showed them to me in his open palm, they hovered a few inches above his hand, spinning counterclockwise.

"You'd be right. This is a training room of sorts for TKs."

"Why spheres?" I asked.

"Because it's cooler than bending metal spoons."

I laughed. "So, the green space isn't just a garden, is it?"

He shook his head. "No, each designation has an area where they can push their abilities. The phytokinetics, geokinetics, and hydrokinetics share the green space. Telekinetics use the atrium, aerokinetics have the aerie—I'll show that to you later—and the electrokinetics have the den, in the basement."

"Why the basement?"

"Electrokinetics deal in electric currents and energies. Pushing their abilities during training tends to short circuit our power systems. They work deep below ground where they're less likely to cause significant changes to our main power structure."

"Are those the only designations here?" He hadn't mentioned mine—pyrokinetics. But maybe there weren't any others like me within the HAC.

The thought was disappointing. I had so many questions I wanted answered. It would have been nice to pick the brain of another psyker with my abilities, maybe get some advice on how to control the pressure when it felt like it was becoming too much.

"No, there are others. Pyrokinetics like yourself, though their space is being renovated. Jax and Cael went overboard a few weeks ago," he said, a wide grin on his face. "They did a lot of damage. We're rebuilding the hot rooms to withstand their abilities. There are others, too, but not here."

The idea of meeting other pyrokinetics, of coming face to face with Jax and Cael, had me practically chomping at the bit, but I didn't want to appear too excited.

"What other designations are there?"

"Chronokinetics, for one. There are rumors of their existence, but I've never met one. We may do some improbable things, but I have a hard time believing that someone out there can mess with time."

"What do you mean?"

"Sorry," he said. "I forget you're still so new to all this. Chronokinetics can go back in time and into the future. From what I've been told, they can only do one or the other. But like I said, I have a hard time believing they even exist."

I wanted to agree with him, but after facing a Chupacabra, I wouldn't ignore the possibility.

"Technokinetics exist, though. They merge their minds with machines. It's pretty amazing, but they can be anti social, spending more time with machines than people."

It was all so much to take in.

"So, Jax and Cael?"

He frowned for a moment. "Cael is on an assignment. But Jax should be here. You'll likely meet him at some point."

"Assignment? What do those entail?" I asked, keeping my voice casual as I pretended to look around the room with interest.

He looked uncomfortable by my question, his hand closing over the three metal spheres in his palm before shoving them into his pocket once more. "It's not important," he said before turning away and exiting the atrium.

"That's kind of vague, don't you think?"

He shrugged his shoulders. I could tell he wouldn't give me anything further, and annoyance flittered through me. I mean sure, in his shoes I wouldn't spill all the beans right out the gate either but he could at least give me something. But seeing a losing battle, I dropped it.

For now.

If I gave him the impression I was open to the idea of the Human Alliance Corporation, maybe in time, he wouldn't be so tight-lipped about things.

As we made our way down the halls, a man approached us.

"Who's this?" he asked Inarus, suspicion stamped across his face.

I looked down at my black boots, grey yoga pants, and short-sleeved tee. I looked like your average twenty-something girl. What was there to be suspicious about?

Okay, so maybe the daggers at my waist and the blood crusting the side of my face wasn't winning me any points, but still, I was harmless.

Usually.

He, on the other hand, looked as if he'd just walked out of a Tomb Raider movie. Dressed in black cargo pants, a black tank top, and some serious military style boots, he looked ready to take on the world.

I took an involuntary step back.

His eyes caught the movement, and a sly smile spread across his face.

"Aria, I'd like you to meet Aiden. He's another TK."

"Don't make me sound so interesting," Aiden chided.

"Aria." He dipped his head. "Nice to meet you." His smile grew into a leer, and I fought to hold his gaze before his eyes dipped to my chest.

Asshole.

He was trying to intimidate me. And he was succeeding. I already disliked him. "So, what do you do here with the HAC?" I asked, ignoring the tension between us.

Inarus gave me a sharp look, but Aiden didn't notice.

"Oh, you know, the usual. A little mischief here, a little mayhem there."

I couldn't tell if he was kidding or not, and from the expression on Inarus's face, neither could he.

"Well, uh, that's interesting," I said.

He laughed, a deep, maniacal sound that grated along my senses. "I'm kidding. I was just dropping off some supplies to one of our hospitals."

"Your hospitals?" I wasn't aware the HAC had any hospitals. In Spokane, we had two that were human run, but I'd consider them closer to science labs for experimentation than health clinics.

"Inarus hasn't told you yet? Our organization funds several hospitals in the Pacific Northwest. I was dropping off some vaccinations for the children's hospital in Wenatchee. Those little kiddos are great. I had to pry them off my legs on my way out. You wouldn't even know any of them were sick."

I had a hard time picturing a bunch of kids warming to the soldier before me. Actually, he reminded me more of a mercenary, which was an insult to my occupation. But I couldn't see him risking his life to defend the free folk. The hospital in Wenatchee could very well be like the ones here, and the vaccines he'd dropped off might be more experimental than preventative.

"So, you guys do charity work?"

He shrugged. "I guess you could look at it that way. Really, we're just looking ahead and planning for our futures, for the next generation." He shot Inarus a knowing look.

There was something he wasn't saying, but if the clench of Inarus's jaw was anything to go by, it was significant.

"So, when are you heading out?" Aiden asked Inarus. "This is the big one before your induction."

Inarus shot him a withering glare.

"Induction into what?"

"Nothing. Come on. Aiden has to get back to work."

"Yep, sure do." He chuckled before heading the opposite direction.

I eyed him suspiciously as he walked away.

"Induction into what?" I repeated.

"It isn't important. Come on. There's more for you to see."

Chapter Fourteen

The following morning, I was ordered down to have breakfast with my mother. It was as I'd expected.

Ridiculously awkward.

I asked Inarus to join us, but he thought it best if I did this on my own. I wasn't so sure I agreed with him, but what choice did I have?

We sat in silence, neither one of us making much eye contact as we ate.

A million questions ran through my head, yet I couldn't get my mouth working to voice even one of them. No, so mom, how ya been? Miss me? Ever think about the daughter you abandoned as a teenager? No? Cool.

God, this was the worst.

She stirred sugar into her coffee, her eyes briefly landing on mine. I opened my mouth to say something, anything, and when words failed me, I shoved toast into my mouth and took a bite to hide my frustration.

She smiled at me like she used to when I was a child, and my heart ached for her approval once again.

I chewed my toasted. It was like gravel going down my throat.

"How are you alive and my father is dead?" I couldn't look at her, so I stared out the balcony window at the snow-littered ground.

The silence was deafening.

Probably not my best opening line, but there was no going back now.

I waited.

And waited.

Finally, I looked at her. Her lips were pressed into a tight line, a furrow between her brows as she considered me.

"I'd been hoping we might reconnect a bit more before delving into such unsavory matters," she said when she finally answered.

Unsavory matters. Was she joking? My father's death was more than just an unsavory matter. Hot indignation coursed through me. "No."

"No?" Her demure expression grew haughty, and an edge slipped into her tone.

"No. He's dead. And you're alive. I've been on my own since I was seventeen, and you were alive the entire time. I'm not waiting to reconnect before getting the answers I deserve."

Anger flared hot in her eyes. Yep, I got my temper from her alright. "I did not raise you to speak—"

I held up a hand up to stop her. "You do not get to lecture me on my manners. Answer the question or I'm leaving. I don't have time for games."

She sat ramrod straight in her chair. Her face marked by the tension in the room. "It's complicated."

"Then uncomplicate it." I gathered my raging emotions, pulling them in and stuffing them down as far as they would go. I'd already grieved my Papa's loss. I didn't need to do it again. "Why were we attacked? Why our family? And why are you still here?" Accusation filled my voice. It should have been her. She should have been the one to die. Not him. Not my Papa.

A part of me couldn't believe that thought had crossed my mind, but staring at the woman across from me only hammered the feeling home.

I didn't believe the sad smile on her face. Not for a single minute.

"Your father knew you were different. That you were a psyker. But at the time we didn't have a name for what you could do. He just called it a power over fire and said his father, your grandfather, had held power over air. He didn't know how to handle your growing abilities. Neither of us did."

I drummed my fingers along the table when she paused, not bothering to hide my impatience.

She sighed dramatically but continued. "He sought outside help. He trusted the wrong people with information about you, what you were capable of." She reached a hand across the table, intending to take my hand in hers, but I jerked out of range.

A flicker of annoyance crossed her face before she hid it behind her mask and folded her hands on the table instead. And that's exactly what it was. A mask.

"They came for you. We were assured they could help. That they could train you and teach you how to control your abilities. But your father refused to let them take you away. I tried to convince him we couldn't control you any longer, that it was the best course of action—but he wouldn't listen."

She was shaking her head now, as though she were reliving an insignificant argument, like whether or not I could have chai with chocolate after dinner. There was no real emotion in her voice. No hint that she'd ever loved him. Or that the thought of losing me had hurt her in any meaningful way.

"When they returned, they came with force and eliminated the obstacle in front of them." Her words were so clinical. There was no inflection in her voice, no remorse, that my father, her husband, had been murdered in front of my eyes.

"You wanted to send me away?" The child inside of me was hurt, even after all these years, to know that she'd been ready to pass me off.

"Sweetheart, you must understand. It was for the best. I didn't know what your abilities encompassed. The damage you could inflict not only on yourself but to others was not inconsequential."

Some mother I'd had. I'd always believed she loved me, would do anything to keep me safe. Really, she was only concerned with her own well-being.

I didn't have any children. I wasn't sure if I ever would. But I did know that if I had a daughter, no matter what the unknown, I'd never give her away to strangers.

"Then what? They killed him, but they never took me." If that was why they'd come—whoever they were—then why leave me behind? "But I saw them take you. I watched you dragged to another room. I heard the gunshot."

She shook her head again. "We—they tried. There was too much fire. You were out of control—"

I slammed my palms against the table. "What did you expect?" Flames burst along my arms to run across my shoulders. "My father was murdered in front of me. Do you have any idea what that did to me? Was I just supposed to stand there and watch it happen without trying to stop it?" Fire filled my gaze. If I didn't get a handle on my emotions, I would lose control. Here and now.

"Control yourself young lady."

"I am not a child you can scold into obedience anymore."

"Aiden." The man I'd met earlier stepped into the room through the open doorway. For a minute, he didn't even look at me.

"Ma'am." With a nod in my mother's direction, he stood at attention waiting for my mother's direction.

"Please help my daughter… control herself."

I shot her a withering glare. And for a split second fear flash across her face. She was afraid of me. Good.

Then I felt pressure. A pushing sensation along my senses.

My eyes shot to Aiden. *Oh, buddy, you have no idea who you're dealing with.*

His eyes were trained on my body and sweat had already beaded on his forehead.

In that moment, I hated him and I let that anger fuel me. He was trying to force my flames back inside of me, and fuck, but it hurt. To hell with that.

I let go of the thin leash I had on my abilities and watched as the flames on my arms grew and spread to the rest of my body. I usually tried to keep my flames caged to my hands and arms—a girl could only ruin so many outfits—but for this instance, I was willing to make an exception.

"Aiden." My mother's voice held a note of worry.

"She's strong," was his reply. "But I've got this."

Wanna bet?

I pushed the flames harder as I pushed away from the table. A layer of fire now covered my entire body from the neck down.

My mother rose as well. "Aria—"

I didn't hear her words after that. Fire raged through me as my blood started to boil, and I kept my entire focus trained on Aiden.

Sweat dripped from his temples and strain bracketed his mouth. His eyes were bright as he pushed his abilities further.

He was strong. He was probably stronger than me. And I knew he was better trained. But none of that mattered. Not when I was this pissed off.

"Why don't you take a deep breath and pull all that pretty fire back inside?" Aiden said.

I held my hands out in front of me and concentrated my flames to form a small ball of fire. It took more effort than I would have liked, but the small sphere formed nearly the size of a baseball. "You'd like that, wouldn't you? But I think I'll pass." The rest of my fire was crushed against my body, small flickers dancing along my skin. But he hadn't been able to push them through yet. All I needed was one distraction. Something big enough to break his focus. Just for a second.

"Sweetheart, you need to calm down before you do something you'll regret."

I scoffed. "Something I'll regret? You really thought you could bring in some lackey to keep me under control—"

"It was just a precaution. I know you still don't have full control over your abilities. I'm only trying to help."

I didn't want her fucking help.

The pressure grew, and for the first time I could ever remember, my body felt like it was going to overheat.

"Make him stop," I said it through clenched teeth, unsure if I'd be able to hold out much longer under the immense telekinetic weight.

I itched to grab one of my blades, but if I lost my focus, he would crush me.

Viola eyed me apprehensively.

"Now!" I yelled. Heat surged through my stomach. A fresh wave of raw power that crashed through me like a tsunami. I'd never felt anything like it before.

The fire along my skin grew, no longer pressed close against my skin. The flames danced along the surface of my flesh, lifting several inches into the air around me.

"Aiden—" she hesitated.

"Now," I ground out again.

My mother nodded, but Aiden looked uncertain.

Hell, I was uncertain. I had pushed myself so hard that if he did let go, it was possible I'd light the whole damn room ablaze.

But if he didn't, if he kept pushing, I was certain it wouldn't be good for me. The pressure was getting tighter and tighter, the heat climbing even higher. Things were going to get bad. Very, very bad and really freaking fast.

"What the hell is going on in here?" Inarus stormed into the room.

I looked at him from the corner of my eye, unable to take my full attention away from Aiden. My skin was overcome by the feeling of pins and needles, and panic swelled in my chest.

"Make him stop." My voice was hoarse, my throat beyond dry. It felt like every ounce of moisture in my body had evaporated.

"If I don't finish this, she'll combust and take us all out."

"Let go. I've got this." Inarus stepped between us, invading my line of sight.

"Inarus…" My mother's tone held an obvious question.

"I've got this."

She nodded in Aiden's direction, and within seconds, the pressure disappeared and my entire body erupted. Fire poured out of me in a rush, followed by a flash of light that illuminated the entire room.

And then the pressure was back. But it wasn't shoving against my fire. It was holding it all in, containing it.

The floor around me was black. A circle of charred hardwood floor stretched four feet out all around me. The table beside me had been within the blast radius, and one corner was sunken in, the wood burnt nearly to ash.

"Take a breath," Inarus said.

I took a lungful of air in through my nose and released the breath through my mouth. I looked up as I took another breath, noticing that despite the high ceilings, there was a scorch mark above me.

"You two should go," he said to my mother and Aiden.

Neither needed to be told twice. Aiden stormed out. His shoulders bunched and anger radiating off of him in waves.

My mother left at a slower, but still hurried pace.

I glared daggers at her retreating form, willing her to trip and fall. Maybe she'd break her neck in the process. If only one could be so lucky.

When both were gone, Inarus came closer. Standing only a few feet in front of me, he reached out and took my hand.

Instinctively, I pulled back, afraid to burn him, but he reached out once more, turning my hand slowly in his to show me no harm was done.

He threaded his fingers with mine, but there was a faint barrier between us.

I realized it was like a force field of sorts. A thin layer protected him from the flames.

"Telekinetic, remember?"

My gaze moved from our connected hands to his eyes, the grey-blue color brighter than I'd seen on him and likely caused by the energy exertion.

"I didn't realize you could do that."

"Comes with being a TK."

"I can't pull it back." I hated to admit that. I hated I had such little control over my abilities right now. But they'd pushed me too far, and my fire was taking over. The flames on my arms were at least four inches high, and the surface of my skin glowed white, an indication I was burning hotter than normal.

His eyes held only understanding. "You can. You just need to focus."

"I can't!" I knew what I could and couldn't do, and this was something I hadn't mastered. I hadn't meditated enough, practiced enough. I didn't have the strength to pull it all in when things raged this far out of my control.

Inarus reached up with both hands and grasped my shoulders, forcing me to concentrate on him. "Try harder."

I closed my eyes and took a shuddering breath. Come on, Aria. You can do this. I mentally snorted.

"Take another breath."

I did as instructed. The only thing keeping me together right now was Inarus's TK. If he released the protective barrier that surrounded me, my flames would cascade in a tidal wave of fire in every direction.

Realizing I didn't have a choice, I did the only thing I could think of.

I listened to him, and I tried harder.

Seconds ticked by, turning into minutes. And Inarus remained patient while I struggled to get a handle over myself. Clearly, he had more patience than I did.

I tried breathing techniques. I tried envisioning the flames receding within my body. I even tried repeating a mantra in my head over and over, anything and everything I could think of to extinguish the flames.

Nothing worked.

Then it hit me, and I cursed myself for not thinking of it sooner. "Can you teleport me while maintaining the barrier?" I didn't love the idea of being teleported, but walking out of here was out of the question.

If Inarus could teleport me to a body of water deep enough that I could submerge myself in it, I could push out my fire until I burned out. All he had to do was keep the pressure on until we got there.

Hope fluttered in my chest until I looked up and met his downcast eyes.

He shook his head. "I'm sorry. I—"

"It's fine." I swallowed the lump in my throat. Now what was I going to do?

Before I could panic more, Inarus gingerly tugged me down to the floor. I let him. Really, what other choice did I have?

We sat cross-legged facing one another, my hands resting in

his. He didn't say anything. He just sat there, exuding calm. He had to have been a monk in his former life.

We sat like that for what felt like an hour before the white-hot flames turned to a red-orange glow.

"See, you can do this."

About damn time. I was so happy, I wanted to cry.

I didn't even care my clothing had been burned away. Or that the only thing protecting my modesty were the orange flames that still coated my body.

I lifted my eyes to meet his, and a smile spread across his face. He gave me a nod of encouragement, and returning his smile, I closed my eyes and concentrated.

Breathe in. Breathe out. Breathe in. Breathe out.

Ten more minutes passed, and when I opened my eyes again, the flames were gone. My fire was still close to the surface, but the flames had receded. I didn't have to worry about burning down the building.

"I did it." I exhaled a breath of relief.

"You did."

Inarus rose and reached down to help me to my feet.

I swayed as I stood, exhaustion hitting me like a train.

He tore off his shirt and helped me into it. Exhaustion tugged at me, my limbs boneless.

"You okay?"

I wiped the sweat from my forehead, my other hand firmly gripped in his to prevent me from falling. "Yeah, I'm okay. Just tired."

"I'll help you back to your room."

I didn't want to go back to my room. I wanted to get out of here. As far away from my mother as possible. But I didn't tell him that.

Instead, I nodded and allowed him to lead me out, each step taking a concentrated effort.

Chapter Fifteen

My cell phone woke me. I didn't even remember turning it
back on.

I didn't need to look at it to know it was Declan calling. I
watched the illuminated screen for several seconds and waited for
the vibration to cease. Less than thirty seconds later, it started up
again. I checked the screen.

This time, the caller was James.

I sighed and stared up at the ceiling. Time to face the music.
"Good morning." I said, keeping my tone light.

"Ari—" the censure in his voice was clear.

"James, I can't. Not right now."

Seconds ticked by in silence.

Was he still there? I looked at the display to be sure. The call
hadn't ended.

"Hello?" I heard voices on the other end but couldn't make
out their words. Who the hell was he talking to?

"I'm not going to get into it with you right now, but can you
at least tell me if you're okay?" he finally asked.

"I'm fine. Why?"

"Because your mate doesn't think you're fine."

"I don't have a mate," I countered, though I tucked away the fact that Declan had known something was wrong. I could still feel him inside of me. But I couldn't decipher his feelings in detail. Was it the same for him, or was he seeing a lot deeper into me than I wanted him to?

"When are you coming home?"

Voices sounded behind the door to the room I was staying in. I tiptoed closer to the door and strained to hear what they were saying, momentarily blocking out James's voice.

"Ari. Are you going to answer me?" James was irritated.

Well, he could join the club.

"I'll call you later. I need to go," I whispered into the phone.

A deep growl rumbled through the receiver. I hung up on him anyway.

"She isn't out of control. She just needs time. Practice."

"She's volatile." I recognized my mother's voice.

Let it all out, mom. Tell me how you really feel.

"You set her off."

"So, this is my fault?"

I rolled my eyes. Her haughtiness was in no short supply.

"You shouldn't have called Aiden in." That was Inarus.

I pressed closer up against the door, careful not to make a sound.

"What was I supposed to do?"

"Things never would have escalated had you let her be. You pushed her. What did you expect would happen?"

I didn't hear what was said next. The door handle jiggled, and I jerked violently away before running back to the bed.

And then I realized that hey, I was a grown adult. I wasn't doing anything wrong. Screw them if they had a problem with me eavesdropping. That was their problem. Not mine.

When the door remained closed, I crept forward again.

"—and the vampire?" I heard my mother ask.

"Unpredictable… Tried killing…" Dammit, I was only getting bits and pieces.

"Remind… the video… keep her in line."

A video? What video? And what vampire? Were they talking about Irina?

"How much does she know?" My mother's voice was closer now.

"She knows enough. You never should have gone after the child."

"Children inspire devotion. Had it been an adult, the result wouldn't have been the same. There is always a price for change."

"He was a child." Inarus's voice dripped with disdain. "That was a line you never should have crossed."

"It was an animal." Indifference colored my mother's words.

How had I never seen the monster she truly was?

Red filled my vision. I wanted to punch her in the face. How could she say that? How could she disregard Daniel's life so completely? I clenched my hands into fists and fought the urge to swing the door open.

"I'm taking her home. You told me you wanted to reconnect with her, but that isn't your goal. You have no intention of being the mother she lost."

"Tread carefully," she warned. "Now isn't the time to lose faith in the cause."

He didn't respond.

The click of heels on tile sounded on the other side of the door, growing more distant with each step.

The door handle turned, and Inarus stepped inside. His brows were furrowed, and his lips were pressed into a tight line. "How much did you hear?"

"Enough."

He ran his hand through his midnight-black hair. "She isn't—"

"A calculating bitch?" I asked.

He shook his head, but looked away. "She wasn't always like this."

"I know. She's my mother. Remember?"

He nodded, but his eyes remained distant. "I should take you home. You were right. I shouldn't have brought you here."

I didn't want to be here, but I couldn't let the opportunity of gathering intel on the HAC and my mother slip past me. And if sleuthing around kept me from dealing with Declan and the mate bond, then that was just the cherry on top of the flipping sunday. "Let's give it a day. I'm beat."

He scowled and looked me over, concern evident in his gaze. Stepping closer, he cupped my cheek in his calloused palm, and without realizing it, I leaned into his touch.

His eyes darkened, and he took another step closer. His gaze moved to my lips.

I pressed a hand against his chest. Whether to stop him from getting too close or to pull him closer, I wasn't sure. What I did know with almost complete certainty was this was a horrible idea.

His heart drummed a steady beat beneath my hand, and I had the sudden urge to slip my hand beneath his shirt to feel the heat of his skin.

"I don't think it's safe for you here." He bent forward and pressed his face against my hair. His free hand reached down to grip my hip and tugged me until my body was flush against his.

Alarm bells went off in my head.

Inarus moved his hand on my cheek to my jaw and tilted my head up to meet his gaze. His grey-blue eyes smoldered. *Actually smoldered.*

This was a bad idea. I needed to step away. I shouldn't— couldn't let this go any further.

"You're so fucking beautiful."

His words made my stomach clench and tension coiled tight inside me. His descent was slow, giving me every opportunity to pull away if this wasn't what I wanted.

But I didn't move. And when his lips pressed softly against mine, my body shuddered.

He took my response as permission and deepened the kiss, crushing my body against his chest as he angled his mouth over mine more fully.

I gasped, giving him the opening he'd been searching for, and his tongue delved in to tangle with my own. Warmth spread through my limbs.

I returned the kiss, my arms coming up to wrap around his neck. This was bad. But it also was good. So good. I needed this. Needed to feel something with someone I chose, even if I was going to regret it later.

Without warning, a flood of rage came over me, so visceral the flames I'd believed snuffed out for the time being threatened to reemerge.

I jerked away with a startled gasp, my hand coming up to cover my lips as I struggled to understand the cause of the emotion.

"What's wrong?"

I shook my head. Fuck. I didn't know.

Rage consumed me, the anger so primal that if I'd had claws, they'd have been fully extended and eager to tear flesh from bone.

Realization dawned on me. These were Declan's emotions. This was his rage. But underneath, I felt the sting of rejection. The bone-deep sense of hurt and betrayal.

God, this was so messed up.

I cursed and looked into Inarus's concerned gaze, taking another step back.

I didn't owe Declan anything. He'd forced me into this. I never asked for it. That he was hurt and angry should have been of no concern to me. But it was.

A chasm had opened in my chest, a feeling of emptiness beginning to take root.

"Aria?" Inarus asked again, reaching out to me.

I allowed him to pull me towards him, shoving down Declan's emotions as I tried to seek comfort in Inarus's arms.

I'd wanted this. Right?

But I couldn't ignore the grief that swept through me. That was Declan's.

But the sudden shame and guilt, that was all my own.

Inarus's touch had elicited a response from me since the day we met. The attraction was clear and obviously mutual. But now, it felt wrong to let another man touch me.

"I don't think I'm ready for whatever this is," I told him.

I could see his disappointment but he didn't push me. "I understand. There's no rush." He gave me a small smile that didn't reach his eyes.

I knew he didn't understand. How could he? He had no idea Declan and I had formed a mate bond, and I had no intention of telling him.

It was probably for the best. I wasn't choosing to stop things with Inarus for Declan's sake. I was stopping for myself. I'd be a fool to let things go any further. He'd already betrayed me once. I couldn't trust him. I mean sure, it was nice to feel a man's touch. To lose myself in tactile pleasure. To let go for once in my life and consequences be damned.

But I didn't need him. I didn't need anyone. At least that's what I told myself.

Chapter Sixteen

Declan

" **G** od dammit," I roared.

How could she let another man touch her? I growled with satisfaction when the table I'd just thrown splintered into pieces against the wall. "How could she do this?" The chairs were next as my fury consumed me. I shredded the fabric cushions with my claws before splitting the frames in two and tossing them aside.

James stepped into the room. His eyes widened as he took in the destruction, but he didn't say anything. He just stood there like a fucking statue.

I ignored him and let loose another thundering roar.

He didn't even flinch. Damn wolf.

"Leave me," I snarled. Clenching my fist, I punched the wall, barely registering the sting in my knuckles as the drywall crumbled beneath my fist. It wasn't enough.

"You're our Alpha. Pull yourself together."

My vision turned red. My beast was on a warpath, and I had no desire to contain it. "I won't warn you again." The wolf obviously had a death wish.

His eyes met mine briefly before looking away. That's right—the tiger is pissed. Best not to make things worse.

Now if he were a good little wolf, he'd turn around and leave the fucking room.

He didn't.

Idiot.

My nostrils flared as I took in his scent, the slight tinge of unease he tried to hide. It wasn't quite fear, but it was enough. My tiger smiled. It wanted the wolf to worry.

James wasn't my enemy, but my beast wasn't happy his feelings for our mate went beyond simple friendship.

He was a potential threat.

If she allowed another man to touch her, who was to say she wouldn't let him? They shared a bond of friendship. And the realization that she cared more for James than she did me tore at my insides and filled me with a jealousy I could barely contain.

My beast urged me to take out the threat. To eliminate all prospective suitors. I shoved those thoughts to the furthest corners of my mind, willing my humanity to the forefront.

I couldn't go around killing everyone who'd ever shown an interest in my mate. Not that my beast gave two shits about what was right or wrong.

All it knew was that Aria was its mate. And Aria wasn't here. It was a problem both sides of me wanted remedied.

"What's going on with you?" James leaned against the doorframe, trying to look calm, but I could see the coiled tension in his shoulders. Knew he was seconds away from lunging should I choose to attack.

I stalked forward, my feet silent as they stepped around the debris scattered throughout the room. Small bits of wood and plastic pierced my bare feet. I ignored the pain. It was nothing compared to the gaping wound in my chest.

"Declan?"

My nostrils flared. His familiar scent reminded me he was Pack.

I shook my head and tried to clear the red haze. "She's with someone." The words came out a guttural growl.

I didn't have to explain further. The pity in James's eyes said he knew exactly what I'd meant with that one statement.

"Where is she?" I paced the room. She was mine. I needed her back. I needed her here. How the fuck was I going to win her over if she wasn't fucking here?

James's shoulders stiffened, and he looked away, unable to meet my gaze.

I narrowed my eyes. He had one job. One fucking job. "I thought you had her followed when she left." That was the only reason I'd let her go. He'd assured me he'd keep a tail on her. What the hell happened?

"I did. Robert followed her, but lost her downtown."

I snarled. "You sent the coyote?"

He gritted his teeth, and a chagrined expression stole over his hard features. "He volunteered. I didn't think she'd be able to lose him." She shouldn't have, but my mate was slippery when she wanted to be. A kernel of pride unfurled in me.

Robert was a shifter. And an Alpha. He better have a good reason for losing my mate. "Find him."

James left, but he wasn't gone long. Less than five minutes passed before he returned with the Alpha of Clan Cadinae.

"Explain yourself."

"She went with the psyker. I can't follow someone that teleports." His tone was dejected. I wasn't buying it.

"She went with him? Willingly?" Was she so desperate to escape this bond that she'd trust the enemy? No. She was angry, not stupid.

"Uhh. Well..." he trailed off and worked his jaw before jerking a hand through his hair and tugging at the short blond strands in agitation.

If the coyote took much longer to answer, I'd take out my remaining aggression on him. "Come out with it already." I growled.

"I followed her downtown. She met with her friend. The harpy woman she used to live next to."

I nodded. I'd met her in passing, and she'd seemed harmless enough. Knowing she'd run to a friend was a good thing. Maybe she'd needed someone to talk to. Women did that. They liked to talk through their feelings. But if she'd gotten everything off her chest, why hadn't she returned?

"And then?"

He sighed and turned toward James for help.

"I've got nothing, man." James raised both hands up in surrender.

"I swear. Your mate has a knack for finding trouble." Robert grumbled. "I followed her after she met with the harpy. She looked like she was going to Sanborn Place, but she caught sight of a vampire and followed her instead."

"What vampire?"

"The Coven's second."

James shook his head. "Fuck. She couldn't help herself, could she?"

Neither Robert nor I answered. It hadn't been a real question anyway. Aria was impulsive. It was one of the many things that drove me crazy about her. But hell, I loved that about her. She always dove head first. She was strong, resilient. Everything my beast wanted in a mate.

A flicker of Robert's coyote filled his eyes, and a primal sense of warning had my tiger rising to the surface. "Was she hurt?"

He nodded. "She had two blood servants. Aria was disarmed, and I was too far away to intervene." He shook his head. Regret stamped across his face. "I would have been too late. I fucked up." Robert growled before he continued. "And then out of nowhere, the psyker appeared. He killed the blood servant who attacked Aria, and before I could do more than shout her name, they were gone."

Was kidnapped? Was this that asshole swooping in and pretending to save the day so he could manipulate her later?

"FIND HER," I bellowed.

Robert didn't need to be told twice. He left the room as quickly as he'd arrived.

James stayed behind. Clearly, he had a death wish.

"She needs space to come to terms with all of this."

And I'd tried giving that to her. But I couldn't ignore the fact she was with the enemy. "She isn't safe. Do you care so little for her that you would abandon her to our enemy?"

James stiffened. "I would never abandon her. But—"

"Then find her. You're my Hunter. Do what you were born to do." My anger subsided, leaving behind a gaping hole where my mate belonged.

Aria wasn't shifter—wasn't like me. She didn't have a beast inside of her, driving her need to be by my side.

There was a chance the bond was one sided. A chance that no matter what I did, she would continue to reject me.

The thought had terror streaking through me.

"I'll try to get her to come back," James said. "But I won't force her. She needs to make the decision on her own. If you take away her ability to choose, you'll only push her farther away. Trust me. She'll come around."

"And if she doesn't?" I leaned against the wall, wanting to trust what the wolf said.

"You can't let yourself go down that road. Not yet."

Easy for him to say. He wasn't the one missing the other half of his soul.

Chapter Seventeen

"Jesus, Ari, it's good to hear your voice."

I'd debated for ten minutes whether I should call James, but I needed my best friend. And I needed answers.

My shoulders sagged, and I heaved a sigh of relief at the lack of anger in James's voice. "It's good to hear yours, too." I hadn't realized how much it sucked, not talking to him these past few days. I was a complete jerk for ignoring him.

"Where are you? I'll come get you."

I shook my head before I realized he couldn't see me. "No. Not yet. I'm not ready to..." I trailed off.

He answered with a growl.

"I'm sorry," I whispered. "I need more time."

He released an exasperated breath. "Will you at least tell me how you're doing?"

"I'm okay. Just trying to get my head on straight." I paused, debating how much to say. I didn't want to worry him but... "I thought all of these strange feelings would go away if I put space between me and Declan."

His voice gentled. "He's your mate. That feeling won't ever go away."

I'd figured that out already, but I'd needed the confirmation.

"Declan's lost. He damn near destroyed an entire conference room with his bare hands."

My breath hitched as my heart plummeted. "I didn't know how deep the bond went. I never in a million years could have imagined he'd know when I…"

"When you let another man touch you?" There was understanding in James's voice, but I didn't miss the frustration. "Your souls are intertwined. If he ever touched another woman, you'd know it too."

The thought of Declan with another woman sent fiery hot rage through me. I'd kill any woman who dared touch him.

It was a visceral truth, and it left me reeling. "God, I'm such a bitch." My feelings where Declan was concerned were a ball of tangled knots I was no where close to unraveling. I didn't want him. But just the thought of him with anyone else… I couldn't think about it.

"Ari, just come home."

"I can't." I interjected before he could argue. "Not because of Declan." Though even I knew that was a partial lie. "I need to learn more about the HAC. And I need to know their strengths and weaknesses if we're going to have any chance standing against them."

James hissed out a breath. "That isn't your job. You're risking yourself unnecessarily."

"If you were in my shoes, would you pass up the opportunity to learn more?"

He swore. "I knew you were with the psyker. But you're in the viper's pit, too, aren't you?"

"I can't pass up this opportunity." My mother was here, and while I had no illusions of becoming one big happy family, I needed to know what she was up to.

I needed to know just how dirty her hands were.

"Be careful and don't go rogue. If you need backup, you call me."

"I will," I promised. "I should go."

"Call him. I know it'll be awkward but… he needs to know you're okay, and his beast needs to hear his mate's voice."

I worried my lower lip. "We don't even like one another. These past few weeks all we ever did was argue."

"That's just verbal sparring in Declan's book. He admires you. Your intelligence, your snarky sense of humor, and your dog-with-a-bone-attitude. He's a crazy bastard, but he's crazy about you, Ari. Don't ever doubt that."

I chewed on my lower lip.

"I've gotta go. I'll talk to you soon." I hung up without giving him the chance to respond and stared down at the phone in my palm.

It weighed heavily in my hand.

"Just get it over with," I muttered to myself.

Before I could second-guess my decision, I pulled up my call log and hit Declan's number.

He answered on the first ring. "Hey."

"Hi." Butterflies filled my stomach as I waited, just listening to the sound of his breathing. The knot in my chest loosened.

"Are you okay?" His deep voiced caressed my senses. "Are you hurt?"

A smile tugged at my lips. "No. I'm fine."

He exhaled a relieved sigh. "Good."

Silence stretched between us. But it wasn't uncomfortable.

I sat on the edge of the bed in the room I'd been given and stared down at my bare feet. There was so much unsaid between us, I didn't know where to begin.

"Do you know when you'll come back?" Hope was evident in his tone.

My stomach clenched and did stupid cartwheels in the pit of my stomach. Did I want to go back? "No. I… umm—"

"I know it's a lot to take in. But, don't say no without at least hearing me out. One conversation in person. That's all I'm asking for."

I considered her. He wasn't being unreasonable. For once. "I can't give you any promises."

"That's okay. I just want a chance to talk. I want you to come home."

Home. I breathed in a shaky breath. "The Compound isn't my home."

"It is. You just haven't realized it yet."

Chapter Eighteen

I spent the next few days exploring the grounds of the HAC, Inarus acting like my shadow. He'd been on edge since his conversation outside my room with my mother and I wasn't sure how to break the tension between us, or if I even wanted to.

He was being cagey, and it didn't take long to realize that while showing me around, there were certain hallways he avoided. I made a mental note of every one of them and filed the information away for later use.

I wasn't an idiot.

And while he'd made it clear he wouldn't lead me in certain directions, I'd made a clear plan to wander them on my own behind his back. I was almost certain he was aware of my plans but he never commented on it one way or the other. Communication had been strained these last few days. An awkward hesitancy between us. I wasn't sure if it was because of the overheard conversation or the kiss. But my money was on the kiss.

We'd both avoided talking about it, which was fine by me. Preferred, actually. But the tension was growing thicker by the day.

I'd been right, assuming I'd later regret it. And sure, it might stem from whatever feelings I had for Declan,—not that I was admitting to any of them being positive feelings—but more so, I regretted the kiss because it wasn't me. Random hookups weren't my coping mechanism. Punching and stabbing were more my style. And while Inarus was still in the unknown category between friend or foe, no one deserved to have their emotions toyed with.

I was certain his feelings for me were genuine. And it made me feel like a complete jerk.

Now as I walked, my boots making soft thumping noises along the tiled floors, I wondered what he would say if he found me right now, wandering around without him. Then I wondered would happen if I was caught by anyone but him.

I mean, what could they do—kill me?

A slight chill ran up my spine as I realized that was a very distinct possibility. And given my latest encounter with mommy dearest, I doubted I was high on her list of people worth protecting. I checked the holsters that rested on my hips, assuring myself that I had my blades, and I had my fire.

I wasn't defenseless.

Pursing my lips, I scanned the barren hallways, taking in the whitewashed walls and fluorescent lights overhead. I passed all the rooms Inarus had shown me earlier this week—the green space, the atrium, the commons, and the kitchen.

No turning back now.

The farther I walked, the sparser things seemed to become, until the hallways took on a clinical feel. A chemical smell in the air made my nose itch. The astringent scent stronger with each step I took toward a large set of metal double doors.

The hairs rose on the back of my neck as I neared.

My instincts roared I wasn't supposed to be here. The urge to turn back coursed through me.

I eyed the door apprehensively. I needed to know what lay

behind that door. Despite wanting to back away, I knew I had to see whatever lay beyond. Had to know just how far the HAC would go to get what they wanted.

I reached for the door handle, ignoring the distinct feeling of being watched. I hadn't seen any cameras. It had to be my nerves talking.

Get it together, Aria.

I turned and looked over my shoulder anyway—the hall leading back the way I'd come was still empty. I checked the ceiling and confirmed again there were no cameras. Nothing to indicate I was being watched. But I still couldn't shake the feeling.

As my hand hovered over the doorknob, I caught a familiar scent.

Rainstorms.

Dammit. I whirled just in time to see Inarus teleport in at my back.

"What are you doing here?" His grey-blue eyes narrowed in suspicion.

"Investigating." I word-vomited out before turning back to the door and giving it a hard jerk, curious to see how far he'd go to stop me.

Inarus slammed his hand against the door, effectively keeping me from opening it. "You shouldn't be here. You don't even know what's behind here."

I rolled my eyes, "Do you?" and folded my arms over my chest.

"This room is above my clearance. Come on. I'll take you down to the green space." He turned to leave. He couldn't possibly expect me to follow.

"Yeah, I'll pass." Before he could stop me, I swung the door wide open.

Chapter Nineteen

Inarus grabbed my arm, the heat from his palm causing small prickles of sensation to shoot into my skin.

"Ari—"

Ignoring the warning in his voice I pulled free from his grasp and stepped inside.

"Fuck. We can't be here." He stepped in front of me trying to block my view before reaching out to take my hand. "Please, we need—"

I dodged around him and then sucked in a horror-filled gasp as my gaze landed on the room.

Everything was white. Tiled floors met bleached walls with laboratory tables in the center of the room. Lining two of the walls were a series of cages. Some were empty, but most weren't. My stomach twisted into knots. What lay before me was eerily similar to what you'd find in an animal shelter only behind some of the bars weren't dogs or cats. No, they were the prone forms of children.

"Oh, my god!"

I covered my mouth as I choked on the words that couldn't begin to describe the horror standing before me.

Upon closer inspection, I could make out a handful of small animals hiding in the back corners of some of the cages. What the hell were they doing with them?

I approached one with cautious steps. A small red wolf shook inside, its fur matted. Its skin hung off of its body. Its ribs sticking out. I could easily count each bone. Bile rose in my throat and my eyes met the wolf's pain filled gaze.

Intelligence shone brightly in the little wolf's eyes. A shifter. Little more than a pup.

I gripped the lock and pulled hard. "We have to get them out of here."

I looked into the next cage. The eyes of a young boy stared out from behind the bars. He couldn't have been over the age of eight or nine. He huddled in the far corner of the cage, arms wrapped tightly around his knees as he rocked himself back and forth.

I tried to reach my hand through the bars towards him, but instead of reaching for me, he curled further into himself, letting out a mewling sound of fear.

My heart clenched.

"What have they done to you?" I whispered.

The boy turned towards me, peeking over his arm to reveal cornflower-blue eyes with a distinctive metallic glow.

Beside him, a boy who looked about five occupied another cage. As soon as I turned my attention toward him, he shifted. His brown hair turned into the thick fur coat of a small brown bear. He struck at the bars with claws and fangs extended. His growl filled with pain as he vocalized his rage.

I swallowed hard and turned to the next one. A girl. Waif-like, her long blonde hair hanging in thin strands around her face, her cheeks hollowed out from a lack of food. She couldn't have been more than four. I crouched in front of the enclosure and reached out to her. "It's okay. I'm here to help."

She eyed my hand with apprehension.

I gentled my voice. "I won't hurt you. No one will ever hurt you ever again." I couldn't image what she'd already been through. The small bear continued to attacked the bars of his encloser and a single tear slipped down my cheek as I tried to encourage the little girl closer.

Inarus shifted his weight behind me.

"Come here, sweetheart," I crooned.

She carefully inched forward, her eyes cautious and her movements hesitant. I noticed her right leg dragged behind her as she crawled my way and bit my cheek to hold back the foul curses I wanted to spew.

How could they do this to innocent children?

Fire burned through my veins. If I didn't get a handle on my emotions, flames would jump from my skin. These children had been through enough. I didn't think they could handle a woman on fire right now.

As she neared, I made a conscious effort to keep my heart rate even. She was a shifter, and I needed to exude calm. I didn't want my anger at her circumstances to upset her beast.

When she was finally close enough, I allowed my hand to tuck a piece of blonde hair behind her ear. She leaned into the touch, rubbing against my palm in a distinctly feline manner. "Smell like home," she whispered in the soft sweet voice of a toddler.

My eyes watered. I blinked several times to clear my vision and wondered if my spending so much time in the Compound was why she'd made the comment. Was she one of the Pack's cubs? How long had her parents been searching for her?

"I'm going to get you out of here. I'll take you home, okay?"

She looked up. Her grey eyes filled with more sorrow and pain than any four-year-old should ever have to endure. But inside their depths, I saw trust. She knew I was telling the truth. And I'd make damn sure I followed through on my promise.

I turned back to Inarus, rage boiling in my blood. "You have to get them out."

Before I'd even finished the comment, he was shaking his head, regret stamped across his face. "Aria, I can't. We shouldn't even be here."

I bit back a curse and curled my hands into fists. "They're just kids. What do you mean you can't? Is it that you can't, or you won't?"

Indecision darkened his face. "We don't know why they're here. There could be a reason—"

I shoved him into a nearby wall using his surprise to my advantage as I got in his face, my nose only inches from his while flames licked across my fingers.

So much for keeping a lid on my abilities.

"There is no reason good enough to take a child. Look at her, Inarus. Really look at her." He turned his head and stared down at the little girl. "Her leg is broken. She's malnourished. There are bruises covering both of her arms. They are torturing them."

"They're shif—"

I cut him off with a hard slap to the face. His eyes hardened, and he brought his hand up to touch the red handprint I'd left on his cheek.

I shouldn't have struck him, but I needed him to wake up and realize the HAC wasn't all sunshine and roses. The HAC weren't the good guys.

"This is where I draw the line. We all have choices we have to make. You said you didn't have anything to do with Daniel's death. You said you would never hurt a child, shifter or otherwise. Prove it."

I heard footsteps in the hallway, and we both froze, eyeing the door warily.

I lowered my voice. "Show me you still have your humanity. Get them out of here." It was a vicious whisper, and I prayed desperately he would listen to me. That he was the man I knew he could be and that my mother hadn't erased his sense of right and wrong.

But he needed to act now. If we were caught before he had the chance to remove the children, any chance of rescuing them would be lost.

He stared down at me, a battle waging in his eyes. When the footsteps in the hallway faded, he clenched his teeth and gave a stern nod, moving to the nearest cage—the one holding the four-year-old girl. I release a breath and watched as he extended his hand toward her, but she drew away from him as the shivers that wracked her body increased.

I rushed toward them. "It's okay," I told her. "We're going to take you home. I need you to let him touch you. Come on, sweetheart."

She shook her head vigorously.

"Please, sweetheart. I won't let anything bad happen to you. He's here to help."

She chewed her bottom lip but carefully drew closer to Inarus's outstretched hand.

"Take her to my apartment."

He nodded, his lips pressed into a thin line. As soon as his fingers met hers, they were gone.

It took thirty-seven seconds for him to come back. I know because I counted. Each one feeling longer than the one before.

I was already in front of the next cage, trying to calm the bear cub into staying still. He swatted at my hand when I reached for him, and I bit my cheek to keep from crying out as sharp little claws ripped into my hand.

Small droplets of blood seeped from the wound, but the little bear's grip put him close enough for Inarus to slide his hand in and grip the scruff of his back.

Then they were gone.

We continued that way through six cages, releasing six children in just over five minutes.

There was only one cage left. Inside stood a teenaged boy, and he didn't look like he had any intention of cooperating.

Rebellion sparked in his gaze.

"We're going to take you home."

"He's one of them." The boy pointed at Inarus.

"He won't hurt you," I assured him.

He shook his head, refusing to move.

I switched tactics.

"He's going to take you to the rest of the children. They need you." It was an asshole move, but I needed him to come closer.

As the oldest, I hoped he would feel responsible for the others. I was banking his shifter's need to protect would outweigh his apprehension.

I wasn't disappointed. The agony in his eyes was heartbreaking. "I was supposed to protect them." His voice was barely above a whisper.

"You still can. Let us take you to them. You can look over them while we find your parents."

The door handle jiggled, causing me to jump out of my skin.

"Hey! You can't be in here!"

Shit. We were out of time. I hadn't even heard the footsteps.

"Aria—" Inarus's hand brushed my shoulder, and I jerked away from him.

"The boy first." I refused to leave him behind.

Inarus reached into the cage, but the boy still refused to come closer.

Dammit.

"He won't let me touch him. We need to go!"

The man who'd just come in stormed toward us. Dressed in a white lab coat, his greasy black hair hung limp around his face.

He looked murderous as he passed the half dozen empty cages. "What have you done? Where are they?" he bellowed.

I let my fire rush over me. It crawled up the length of my arms to cover my shoulders.

I widened my stance and faced the enemy head on.

With a swift motion of his hand, tables flew across the room, giving him a clear path to me.

Shit! He was a TK. This wasn't good. If he was as strong as Inarus, my fire wouldn't do a damn bit of good against him.

I pushed my fire into the shape of a ball and threw the flames his way.

He stopped for only a second, an invisible shield forming before him that my flames pressed against before sliding off like water pouring over a stone.

I threw another one, forcing him to shield himself again, unable to advance forward. The distraction wouldn't last long.

"Get him out of here!" I yelled to Inarus.

Chancing a glance behind me, I saw that Inarus and the boy were gone. I heaved a sigh of relief. He was safe. All the children were safe. I only had a moment to celebrate my victory before I was thrown backwards.

My back hit the metal bars of an empty containment cell, and a sharp stab of pain shot down my spine.

Before I could recover, I was yanked to my feet by an unseen force, the furious man stalking toward me as I hung suspended in the air. I clawed at the invisible hand holding me by the throat but found no purchase. My eyes bulged, and I kicked wildly in the air as I struggled to breathe.

"Where did you take them?" His face was mottled with rage, spittle flying from his lips.

I clawed at the air, desperate to escape. But it was no use. I choked on my own saliva and black spots darkened my vision.

"Tell me, and I'll make this quick. Lie to me, and I'll show you fates worse than death." His eyes held a manic gleam.

I tried calling my fire again, but the lack of oxygen made it hard to concentrate. Even if I'd wanted to answer him, I couldn't.

Before darkness consumed me, I was dropped to the floor. Unconsciousness pulled at me and I fought to stay awake. It was a losing battle but before the dark consumed me, I felt a familiar tug in the pit of my stomach and gasped.

Fuck. I'd never been so happy to be teleported in my life.

Chapter Twenty

Surrounded by small children and fur-covered shifters, I sighed in relief and did a head count. The four-year-old girl —the smallest of the bunch—was tucked beneath my chin in her human skin, a contented purr coming from her chest.

My eyes roamed the room, recognizing the pale cream walls and olive-colored comforter. We were in my apartment. But Inarus was nowhere to be found.

A creak to my right had me turning my gaze toward the teenage boy we'd rescued. He stared at me through the eyes of a predator. His metallic copper gaze locked on mine.

I held his stare, refusing to look away. He needed to know I was in charge. I was the more dominant of the two of us. I also knew I was in no condition to fight. I didn't want to hurt him. And given my current state, if he decided to strike, I had little chance of defending myself with the young ones surrounding me.

After a minute passed, he looked away. I exhaled a relieved breath before I pushed myself into a sitting position. I did my best not to disturb the little ones, smiling at the small growls and grumbles that erupted around me for daring to disturb their slumber.

They all settled back quickly enough, and I found myself combing my fingers through the hair and fur of several children.

"How long was I out?"

"Less than an hour."

Had he stayed in that seat the entire time? "And the man who was with me?"

The boy shrugged his shoulders. "He left without a word after laying you down."

I frowned. "Did he leave a note?"

He shook his head.

I chewed my lower lip. Not much I could do about that. If Inarus wanted to see me, he knew where to find me. He was probably just blowing off steam after being forced to help me. He'd get over it. Deep down, he had to know this was the right choice.

I pulled my cell phone from my back pocket and dialed Declan's number. My heart raced and my stomach churned as I waited for him to answer. It took five rings before he picked up.

"Aria?" Relief filled his voice.

I rubbed at the ache that suddenly formed in my chest. "Hi…" I paused and took a deep breath. "I need…"

"Anything. All you have to do is ask."

"Can someone pick me up at my apartment?"

"I can be there within the hour."

"I have children. Eight of them." I added. "We won't all fit in one vehicle."

He didn't miss a beat. "Brock is in the area. He can be there in ten minutes. I'll be there shortly after."

"Okay."

"Stay put. Promise me." I heard the desperation in his voice. And it was one promise I couldn't deny him.

"I won't go anywhere. I'll see you soon." Hanging up, I tucked my phone back into my pocket.

"That was my Alpha." It was a statement, not a question.

Damn that shifter hearing.

"You carry his scent." He tilted his head to the side and scrutinized me. "But you're not Pack?"

How was I supposed to respond to that?

"You're my Alpha's… mate?" He seemed confused and I couldn't blame him. Shifters didn't take human mates. Wives, sure. Mates, not so much. At least not that I'd ever heard of.

I nodded in confirmation. No sense denying it if it would make him more comfortable.

He stood from his chair and kneeled before me, his eyes wide but directed towards the floor. "I'm sorry. I shouldn't have disobeyed. I didn't know. I shouldn't—"

"Hey. Shh… It's okay. Everything is going to be okay now. We're going home." I touched his shoulder, and it seemed to settle him. He leaned into my touch, and I took a moment to run my fingers through his hair.

"What's your name?"

"Caden."

I nodded and tugged him onto the bed beside the rest of the children. "Well, Caden, the cavalry will be here soon. For now, relax. All of us are going home."

Chapter Twenty-One

True to Declan's word, Brock arrived ten minutes later.

He took in the malnourished and injured children with a hard stare. His cognac eyes were bright, his lion close to the surface.

And then our resident bear cub launched himself into Brock's arms, and his hard expression evaporated into tenderness.

He ran his fingers through the cub's rich brown fur and nuzzled him close to his cheek. "How can I help?" He asked, his eyes still on the cub in his arms.

I couldn't help the smile that tugged at my lips. "I'm sure everyone's hungry. I don't have much here, but there should be fixings for peanut butter and jelly."

He nodded. "I can do that."

Not putting the cub down, he strode toward the kitchen and propped him on his shoulder, trusting that the cub would manage to hang on while he went about making the sandwiches.

I watched him from across the room and admired the care he took with the small boy, adjusting his stance and angling his shoulders back. Small things, but they made it easier for the cub to maintain his grasp.

With Brock on peanut butter and jelly duty, I took a seat on my sofa beside Caden while we waited for the rest of the cavalry to arrive.

The four-year-old we'd rescued carefully pulled herself into my lap. She'd shifted into her animal form—a were-lynx—after waking up, able to move around better on four legs than two. Her leg had healed at the wrong angle after having been broken, but she managed to crawl around without too much effort while in her animal form. It would have to be broken again to realign it. Hopefully the Pack doctors could put her under for the process.

Brock came into the living room with a plate full of sandwiches he'd neatly cut into triangles. Setting them on the coffee table, he took a seat on the floor across from me. The bear cub settled into his lap, and Brock held out a sandwich for him.

He dutifully took it in his paws and shoved it into his mouth, smearing peanut butter along his nose in the process.

Caden laughed. "His name is Tito in case you're wondering."

"Tito, huh?" He picked him up under his arms and held him out in front of his face. "Well Tito, I think you and I are going to get along great."

Tito wiggled in Brock's grip and made a small, but happy, growl.

"And you are?" Brock asked Caden. There was a gleam of interest in his eyes.

It made sense. Caden was a werelion like Brock. The two would likely be getting to know one another over the coming days.

"Caden—" He nodded in Brock's direction. Man-speak for 'Hi. Nice to meet you.'

I hid a smile behind my palm and gave a casual roll of my eyes. "Caden, why don't you introduce everyone."

He shrugged his shoulders. "Sure. That's Penny," he indicated the were-lynx in my lap.

I stroked her silky fur and listened to her soft purr.

"Jeb and Jordan are the two wolf pups. They're brothers. This is Yuli," he indicated the small boy huddled near his legs. "He's a bear like Tito but polar, not brown."

Brock and I gave Yuli a cursory glance. That would explain the white blond hair and jet-black eyes. I'd assumed he was a white tiger like Declan given his hair color, but the eyes were unlike anything I'd seen before. Pitch black with no discernable pupil.

I reached out a hand to him, and he scrambled up from the floor to squeeze between me and Caden. "You don't need to be afraid," I reminded him.

Piercing eyes met mine. He nodded, but he was still shaking.

"Our little fox is Suzie," Caden continued. "And last but not least is Xavier." He waved toward the little boy who sat beside my living room window. He hadn't bothered to acknowledge Brock, but I didn't think it was out of fear.

His eyes had been glued to the window since we'd left my bedroom. I could only image how long he'd been caged. How long he'd gone without seeing the sun.

We coaxed all the children to eat at least half a sandwich. Penny had a hard time keeping the food down, her small body rejecting it at once.

"Shh… It's okay." I held her close and rocked her back and forth in my arms.

My apartment door swung open, and I jumped as the door banged loudly against the wall.

None of the children started, and Brock looked as relaxed as ever when I glanced his way.

"You could have knocked," I chided.

James didn't answer. His grey eyes took in each child before closing in on Jeb and Jordan. His nostrils flared, and he sucked in a breath, his eyes widening. "Jeb? Jordan?"

Both wolves shifted into their human skins, and two tiny naked toddler boys ran full tilt toward James.

"Uncle James!" They shouted.

James bent down and opened his arms, scooping them both up and hugging them close. I sent a questioning look in Brock's direction and mouthed Uncle James?

I hadn't met any siblings of James's, though I supposed that didn't mean he didn't have any.

"No blood relation. But they're wolves. It's not a surprise James knows them."

I nodded.

Setting the boys down, James turned toward me. "I don't know how you found them." He was shaking his head as each boy took one of his hands in theirs. "They're pack. My pack." He was referring to Clan Wolf. "Their father went… I had to…"

"You don't need to explain. I know." I said, not needing him to continue in case he said anything that would upset the boys.

He was the Pack's Hunter. And when James was pushed into action, it was usually to track down a shifter gone rogue and end his life. There wasn't any other way. Going rogue meant you'd lost all humanity and killed without cause or remorse. There was no coming back from that.

"We never found them. There was blood everywhere. I searched with several others for more weeks that I can count just to be sure. We assumed they'd been—" He bit off the words and looked away as his eyes glossed over.

He'd assumed their rogue father slaughtered them.

"It wasn't your fault," I told him, needing him to see that. He couldn't have known they'd been taken by the HAC. He'd had no reason to suspect they were still alive.

He nuzzled the boys before standing back up. "Uncle Tegan and Uncle Derek are going to be so excited to see you."

The boys both made excited sounds before they shifted back into their wolf forms and scampered around the room with yips and growls full of delight.

James and Brock turned their attention toward my open apartment door, and all the children stilled.

Declan filled the doorway.

Dressed in worn jeans and a faded green shirt, Declan would have looked almost casual if it weren't for the predatory stare he directed my way.

My body went motionless, unable to move under his scrutiny.

His emerald eyes gleamed in the light, drawing my attention to his face.

I'd expected him to be angry when he saw me. But it wasn't anger I saw in his eyes. It was concern and a tenderness I was almost certain was directed at me.

But I also saw exhaustion. Dark shadows smudged the skin beneath his eyes, and his hair was a wild and unruly mess.

As we stared at one another, the pit that formed in my chest whenever I thought of him grew into a chasm so wide it seemed endless. The ache was a psychical one, and I had to fight the urge to rub my hand over the emotional wound that felt so raw.

"Hi." I didn't know what else to say.

"We'll get the kids loaded up," Brock said to no one in particular. He and James herded the children out of the apartment with Caden helping to carry Penny.

As each shifter child passed Declan, he paused long enough to pull them into a quick embrace and take in their scent. Each child—even Caden who'd been mostly reserved up to this point —had tears in their eyes as Declan made sure to offer them all physical comfort and assurance that they were safe and heading home.

I saw just how much Declan loved every member of his Pack. What would it feel like to be loved like that?

After everyone was gone, Declan carefully closed the door behind him. The snick of the door loud in the sudden silence.

I'd remained on the sofa. I wasn't sure where we went from here. And judging by Declan's expression, he didn't know either.

"Are you okay?" He moved closer but didn't take the seat beside me. Instead he crouched down in front of me until our gazes were level.

I nodded.

He reached out to cup my cheek.

Instinctively, I pulled away, and hurt filled his expression.

I wanted to smack myself. "I'm sorry. I didn't mean—" I looked away for a moment trying to find the right words to say.

"No. Don't apologize. I'm aware I haven't earned the right to touch you. We don't share skin privileges."

I looked down and my hands. "I'll explain what happened—how I found them—later. Right now…" Right now, what? Did I want him to leave? Did I want him to stay? Was I going to go back with him?

Indecision weighed heavily on me. Had it not been for the children, I'd still be back at the HAC. I'd still be with Inarus. Not *with him* with him. But not with Declan, either. I hadn't been ready to come back before.

I wasn't sure I was ready to deal with this bond between us. Or if I'd ever be ready.

"We don't have to figure everything out right now. No final decisions have to be made. For now, just come back with me."

I pressed my lips together, not trusting myself to speak. I wanted to go with him. Now that he was here, crouched in front of me, everything inside of me sang. But this wasn't normal.

My head warred with my heart.

Deciding to take a leap, I nodded.

Hope filled Declan's expression. But rather than reach out again, he clenched his hands into tight fists as he rose.

I knew he was keeping himself from touching me. I could feel his need through the bond. It was a deep hunger filling me with longing.

I felt that same need within myself.

Not giving myself the chance to second guess it, I stood up and carefully reached for his hand, sliding my palm into his.

He froze.

I waited to see what he would do. If he'd say anything.

Instead, he looked down as he twined our fingers together. And a wave of contentment washed over me.

A smile tugged at his lips, and he pulled me forward, careful to keep me close to his side. "I'm glad you're coming home."

I couldn't help the butterflies in my stomach at the thought of the Compound being my home. But the more I thought about it, the more it felt right.

We were going to have bumps in the road. A lot of them.

And I still had a lot to do. I had a business to run, a mother and an organization to take down, a vampire to kill, and…

It was a lot. Having a love life wasn't something I was ready to take on. But the bond vibrated between us, and I was hopeful Declan would give me the space I needed. We still didn't know one another. And I still hated the idea of being bound to someone.

But I was making the promise to myself that I'd give this a chance.

Like he'd said, we didn't have to figure everything out right now. I would just take things one day at a time.

Aria's story continues in
BURNED BY FIRE
Blood & Magic: Fireborn - Book 3

Grab your copy now on Amazon
Turn the page for a sneak peak—

TWENTY-TWO

Burned by Fire

Chapter One

Being a business owner was a pain in the ass.

If I didn't think I was overworked and underpaid before, I certainly believed I was now.

Sanborn Place was busier than ever, and it was beginning to take its toll. I was hard-working, efficient, some might even say responsible. Okay, no one would ever say I was responsible, but still, I carried my weight, and I got the jobs done. But Sanborn Place was never intended to be a one-woman show. And despite my best efforts, that was exactly what it was right now.

Mike Sanborn—my former boss and mentor—had been brutally murdered by a group of vampires that'd been after me. He'd been in the wrong place at the wrong time and got caught in the crosshairs. It sucked. I'd lost my mentor, my employer, and if I was being honest with myself, I'd lost a father figure. *Again.*

He'd left Sanborn Place to me in his will— not that I'd

deserved it. But for some strange reason he had, and I was determined to do right by his legacy.

Rebuilding the business after I'd all but burned it to the ground—along with the vampires who'd killed him—was the easy part. Keeping up with the clients streaming in through the door was more difficult. I desperately needed to hire another mercenary, or three, but finding good people was proving to be difficult.

Nico Salgado and Taylor Baired had been the only other mercenaries employed on a full-time basis by Sanborn Place prior to Mike's passing. They'd also both been my seniors. Neither had taken me seriously. And when I'd reached out to them with the offer of continued employment, they'd both erupted into continuous laughter. Three straight minutes of it with no end in sight, so I hung up. I didn't need them.

Only I did.

Determined to succeed, I put a job listing in the paper and waited for resumes to come in.

Jack had been my first hire. All muscle and smooth confidence. His resume had been impressive. He was a war veteran. Served three tours overseas. I'd had really high hopes for him. Until I'd sent him out to deal with a little snake infestation problem. The client had been a bit vague on the details, but Jack had assured me he could handle it. He wasn't afraid of a little snake. How hard could it be?

He'd returned forty-five minutes later, handed me his keys to the building, and quit.

Turned out our little snake problem happened to be a six-hundred-pound anaconda, and Jack had no desire to be mistaken for a two-hundred-pound mouse.

I didn't know what the big deal was. Some asshole had imbued the snake with magic. Big deal. With six-hundred pounds of weight, it'd be slow. And snakes weren't known for their intelligence. A few calculated strikes of my blade and a bit of fire, and the whole ordeal was over in no time.

Russell had been hire number two. He had magic. I wasn't sure what kind, but I knew it was there because my skin prickled with awareness whenever he was close. He also had martial arts training, even better. But he broke his ankle while chasing after a demented cat that looked freakishly like a bunny, except for the pointed ears and long tail. Our client called it a "cabbit", a cross between a cat and a rabbit.

Clearly, he wasn't the creative sort when it came to names.

The escapee—Thumper, (See? Again, not very creative)—was his stud cabbit and was *supposedly* worth thousands in potential offspring. We'd been paid a hefty fee to track Thumper down, and despite a broken ankle, Russell completed the mission.

I'd been optimistic, but the broken ankle ultimately put him out of commission. Magic aside, he still healed like any other human. Which was why I'd been working solo this past week. My bank account, not to mention my reputation, couldn't afford to turn down business.

But I was beginning to reconsider that notion as I trudged up the stairs to my apartment, chilled to the bone, wet as a dog, and hungry. My stomach took that opportunity to growl like a bear before plummeting as if trying to flee through my feet. I shook off the queasy sensation that struck me. Food. That's all I needed, and I'd feel like my normal self again.

That and coffee. Copious amounts of coffee.

Water sloshed in my boots as I wiped wet tendrils of my hair away from my cheeks, ignoring the gelatinous goo that slid through my fingers as I tucked my hair behind my ear.

Just another reminder of today's adventure.

I'd had the pleasure of bodyguard duty for one of Sanborn's regulars. I should have been thrilled with the repeat business, but guarding Laela Drucano was a bitch. The job, not the girl.

Then again, she could be one too if she wanted to be.

She was a spoiled water nymph. The apple of her father's—Alexander Drucano—eye. And I, well, I was her glorified babysitter.

The cabin she'd been "vacationing" in was mere feet from the Spokane River. And bored after I'd repeatedly chased off her many male suitors, she decided to screw with me. Royally. It was my job to stick to her like glue. And clearly, it'd been hers to make me miserable. In the middle of January that made for frigid waters and a bone-chilling breeze. And I'd taken the polar bear plunge more than once today. I shook from head to toe and my teeth clattered as I climbed the stairs to my fourth-floor apartment. Only one more flight to go.

Think warm thoughts.

I could already taste the smooth, rich coffee on my tongue and feel the soothing spray of a warm shower against my skin.

As my apartment door came into view, the hairs on the back of my neck rose and my body went on high alert. Something was off, and dammit, wasn't that just my luck.

Scarlet drops made a path down the hallway leading to my door. They stuck out like a sore thumb against the beige carpet. This couldn't be good.

I took a deep breath and debated just turning around. I was too tired to deal with anything else today. Was it too much to ask for some dry clothes and a hot cup of coffee? For chrissakes, I'd take a cold cup of coffee at this point.

Then again, it was my apartment and with my luck, there would be a dead body inside, and I'd be framed for the murder. Why couldn't stuff like this happen at a decent time of day when I was fully rested?

I pressed my ear against the door. Well, really it was more like I slumped against the door, but the result was the same. The wooden door was cool against my cheek and I let my eyes close for a brief moment.

Shit. Snap out of it, Aria!

I jerked to attention and listened for any signs of movement. Silence greeted me. *Maybe there really was a dead body*, I mused with a sick sense of morbid curiosity.

I gripped the doorknob and turned it, careful to go slow and make no sound. The door opened on silent hinges and I peered inside. Bloodied footprints left a pattern across the tiled floor leading down the hallway. The prints were large, clearly a man's. They smeared across the floor as though whoever had walked in had struggled with each step they took. Splashes of crimson handprints painted the walls.

I studied the scene for a brief moment. Whoever had come in was tired and injured.

Well, that made two of us, except for the injured part. I doubted with this much blood loss they would be much of a threat, but I wasn't going to take any chances. Because whoever was here—despite clearly being injured—had managed to break in without breaking any doors or windows. That meant only one thing.

Magic.

My heart pounded in my chest, and adrenaline coursed through my veins. I forced my frozen fingers to withdraw my daggers from the sheath resting low on my hips as I stepped farther inside. I tried to call my fire to the surface, but fatigue made it hard to focus.

Dammit. I needed a nap, food, and a hot shower before I'd be able to conjure up even a spark.

A rustle of movement in my bedroom pushed every one of my senses to high alert. My frozen fingers forgotten, I padded down the hall as silently as my water-filled boots would allow and crept around the corner. Standing in the open doorway, I surveyed my bedroom.

Blood was streaked across the floor and walls and covered my olive-green comforter. Christ, there was so much blood; you'd think Hannibal Lecter had decided to come over for dinner.

My boots made a squishing sound on the carpet, and when I looked down, I realized that I wasn't sure if the sound came from my shoes, or the blood now soaking the floor. The sound of running water caught my attention, and I turned to the adjoining bathroom. Light escaped from beneath the closed door and a shadow moved in front of it.

Yep. The fucker was still here. I debated storming in, or waiting for the intruder to come out on their own. Before I could decide, the bathroom door swung opened. I braced myself to charge when a familiar face greeted mine.

Inarus?

A deep indigo bruise marred the right side of his jaw, and his bottom lip was fat and swollen. Dark purple circles rested beneath both of his stark grey-blue eyes.

What the hell?

Without thought, I lobbed a dagger at his chest. He jerked up his hand, palm out, effectively stopping my dagger midair with telekinesis. With a wave of his hand, the blade landed harmlessly on the ground before he slumped against the doorframe.

I bent to retrieve my dagger as Inarus stared down at me in silence. His expression a mix of brooding arrogance and exhaustion. Sheathing both blades, I folded my arms across my chest and gave him another once over.

He looked like shit.

His jet-black hair was overgrown, the stubble along his jaw at least a few days old. And though he'd clearly scrubbed his hands and arms clean, his low riding denim jeans and light grey thermal shirt were streaked with blood. The large smear of crimson across his abdomen seemed to still be spreading through the fabric of his shirt as he stood there, looking like a strong wind could blow him over.

"What the hell happened to you?" I bit out the words and held myself immobile, even though everything in me screamed to reach out to him. To step forward and offer help he so obviously needed. I dug my nails into my palms and fought the urge to touch him. He wasn't mine. We weren't a thing. And I didn't want us to be. So, why did it hurt to see him like this?

It'd been weeks since I'd seen Inarus. Weeks since he'd helped me rescue a group of shapeshifter children from a lab inside the Human Alliance Corporation. Weeks since I'd guilted him into porting them out of their cages one by one as I had my ass handed to me by the worker who'd stumbled across us before we'd managed to get everyone out. When Inarus came back for me, I'd blacked out. And when I'd woken up, it was in my own bed, surrounded by kits and cubs with no sign of him anywhere. He'd vanished without a word. No goodbye. No explanation. Nothing.

I'd called. I'd texted. He'd completely ghosted me and now he was in my apartment covered in blood.

He had a lot of explaining to do.

"What happened to you?" he countered, waving his arm at the mess that was my current state.

I pushed my hair back behind my ears, my fingers landing on something slimy. I pulled a glob of green sludge out of my hair and tossed it to the floor. *Gross.*

"Water nymph. I was on the job. Your turn." I raked my fingers through my waist-length brown hair to see if more of the river's contents had lingered.

All clear.

Inarus ran his hand through his midnight-black hair, his clear grey-blue eyes filled with a mixture of pain and frustration. "I had a run-in with Aiden. It's nothing."

It didn't look like nothing. It looked like Inarus had his ass handed to him and that in and of itself was surprising. With ropes of corded muscle over a tall lean frame, years of martial arts training under his belt, and TK abilities, Inarus was no push over in a fight.

"What do you mean, you had a run-in with Aiden? I thought he was your friend? You two work together." At least they had. Aiden was one of the HAC's henchmen and at the bottom of my favorites list. Still, I'd gotten the impression that he and Inarus were close.

"I don't have friends. Not anymore."

Well, didn't someone sound bitter?

I knew why I didn't like Aiden—he'd tried putting a leash on my abilities. And I knew why he didn't care for me—he thought I was a danger to others.

I was certainly a danger to him if we crossed paths again.

But what I didn't understand was why Inarus no longer considered him a friend when they were practically besties the last time I'd seen them together.

"I lost everything." He laughed, but the sound was devoid of humor as he stared out toward my bedroom window. Strain etched into the harsh line of his jaw.

I chewed on my bottom lip and read between the lines. He'd lost everything because of me. The repercussions of Inarus helping me rescue the shapeshifter children came into full view. He'd belonged to the Human Alliance Corporation. His life and career was with them. How could I have been so stupid as to expect everything would go on as normal after he went against them to help me?

I opened my mouth—to say what, I had no idea. Did I apologize? Did I ask if I could help or fix this?

I closed it before I could do either of those things. I wasn't sorry. The HAC was shady as hell. They'd kidnapped children for chrissakes. He should be happy he'd gotten out.

But judging by the look on his face, he didn't see it that way.

So instead, I asked the only other thing I could think of. "What are you doing here?" Of all the places he could have gone, why come to my apartment? I was the reason he was in this mess in the first place. He probably hated me.

He sighed. "I didn't have anywhere else to go. They've staked out all of my properties and tied up all of my funds. I figured you'd have some supplies to help me patch myself up. I wasn't planning on staying long."

I looked at him, really looked. "Where'd all the blood come from, Inarus?" the stain on his abdomen was still blooming and I was beginning to worry.

"It won't be long until they track me down again. I'm sorry about the mess. I'd stay and clean up, but it'll be better for both of us if I just leave." Inarus pushed off from the doorway and I followed him as he made his way down the hallway.

"I don't care about the mess. Look, that back there,"—I waved my arm behind me—"it's a lot of blood. I'm—"

He stumbled and caught himself on the wall.

I rushed forward and pulled his arm over my shoulders, taking on some of his weight. His face was frighteningly pale, the purple and blue bruises standing out in a patchwork of color.

I helped him walk the rest of the way to the living room and lowered him onto my sofa. "Look, I'm sorry. I never meant—"

He cut me off. "You didn't do this, Aria."

I shook my head. This was my fault. I didn't regret rescuing the shifter children, but this… I should have known what was going on. I should have been there to help him from the beginning. Guilt tore a hole through me, and I rubbed my chest, wishing I could lessen the feeling.

Inarus leaned back, his hand resting on his stomach. I pushed his hand aside and lifted his shirt, peeling the wet material away from his skin. A hiss of pain escaped him.

I swore. "Shit. This is bad."

An angry gash ran from the right side of his rib cage, curving over to the left and down to his hipbone. The edges were red and swollen. He'd crudely stitched himself together, but the sutures weren't holding. Blood seeped through the wound in rivulets down his muscled torso to settle in the lines between his abdominal muscles.

Inarus pushed his shirt back down, hiding the injury. "I'm fine. It'll heal."

Idiot. Just because he healed faster than a human didn't make him invincible.

"Wait here," I ordered.

He shook his head. "I need to go." Inarus leaned forward, but I shoved him back with a hand on his shoulder.

"Stay put." I glared at him before stepping away. When he stayed put like I'd ordered, I rushed into the kitchen and pulled the first-aid kit from beneath the sink. I had at least half a dozen of them throughout my apartment. I set it on the coffee table and then grabbed a bowl of warm water and a washcloth.

Inarus glared at me through hooded eyes but said nothing as I pushed his shirt up once more. He might not have wanted my help, but he needed it.

I took the washcloth and dipped it into the bowl of warm water before carefully cleaning any excess blood from around the gash. It didn't take long for the bowl of clear liquid to turn a rust red, and I had to dump and refill it two more times.

"Are there any others?" I asked, praying that there weren't. *How was he still functioning with a wound like this?*

"This is the worst of it."

I nodded and then, as gently as possible, went about cleaning the injury itself. His abdominal muscles flexed beneath my hands, but he didn't make a sound. It had to hurt like hell, but he held himself immobile.

I looked up, my eyes meeting his. His skin was still pale, now taking on an ashen quality, and a thin bead of sweat ran down the side of his face. His jaw clenched, his eyes filled with pain, but in his gaze, I saw the unspoken appreciation.

"I don't have any painkillers," I told him. Drugs were scarce these days, and all I had were a few Tylenol, which wouldn't be enough to even take the edge off.

After the Awakening, big pharma had gone under, along with most hospitals, police forces, fire departments, and anything else that our government had supported. The world was rebuilding, but we were a long way away from pharmaceuticals becoming widely available again.

"I can handle it," he gritted out through clenched teeth.

I wasn't so sure about that. His eyes were at half-mast. He was on the verge of passing out.

"I'm sorry I caused this," I said, and I was. "If they're so angry over what we did—" I stressed the "we," because I'd been there too, "—why are they only coming after you?"

Things had been quiet on my end for once. I'd kept busy with mercenary work at Sanborn Place, and James, my werewolf best friend, had done his best to fill my free time with workouts meant to make me as close to shapeshifter strong as possible.

I'd been spending most of my nights at the Compound since Inarus and I had parted ways. Being mated to the Alpha of the Pacific Northwest Pack would probably make someone hesitate before striking out against me, too. But I wasn't unreachable. And last I checked, the HAC didn't care about my mate status.

I stopped in at my apartment at least once a week, and I didn't bother having security or an escort with me—despite Declan's insistence—so why had only Inarus been targeted?

I set aside the rag and pulled out a surgical needle, antiseptic, and thread.

"I'm going to sew over your existing sutures." I told him, "You'll have an ugly scar, but the wound will be sealed, and you'll be able to heal more quickly."

Eyes closed, he nodded.

It worried me that his wound was still bleeding, and that the bruises hadn't started to fade yet. He'd likely burned himself out during his altercation with Aiden, but poison was always a possibility too.

I gently poked at the surrounding flesh. No green tinge. No gross puss or fluids.

I still didn't like it.

Inarus needed food and sleep to recharge. If I could keep him from bleeding out, he should be good to go after a day or two of rest at most, assuming the laceration was the only big issue here.

"Go ahead." His shoulders stiffened before he forced himself to relax.

"I don't need to tell you that this is going to hurt like a bitch."

Inarus huffed out a laugh and winced at the resulting pain before closing his eyes again. I used gauze to apply the antiseptic and then disinfected the needle before threading it. It'd been a while since I'd stitched anyone up beside myself. Hopefully, I wouldn't screw this up.

"So, why are they only after you?" My hand shook slightly as I started. I took a deep breath and then sank the needle into pliant flesh, pulling it through before tugging to ensure the thread would hold. Satisfied, I pushed the needle through again, crossing over the wound in a zigzag pattern.

"You're Viola's daughter. She still hopes you'll join the HAC. You're also not the one with insider information. I'm too much of a liability to let live." He said it so matter-of-factly. Like he'd already accepted his fate.

Anger burned through me. "You've been dedicated to the HAC for years. Why kill you when it would make more sense to keep you as an asset?" My eyes focused on the task at hand until Inarus cupped my jaw and tilted my face towards his. I froze when our eyes connected and stared into twin pools of blue-grey water.

"Aria, does this look like they want me alive?"

I blinked and shook my head. There was resignation in his voice. He thought this was a losing battle.

I gritted my teeth and stabbed the needle back through his flesh harder than I'd intended. He sucked in a harsh breath but said nothing.

His attitude needed to change.

"I'm not going to let them kill you." It was a promise.

His jaw tightened.

I didn't need to say anything else. I kept sewing him back together, focusing on the task at hand instead of on his hardened expression. The sooner he accepted my help, the better.

If my mother wanted to come after the people I cared about, she would have to go through me first. Sure, Inarus had left without even a single goodbye. And yeah, I was still bitter about it. But he was one of *mine*.

Aria's story continues in
BURNED BY FIRE
Grab your copy now on Amazon

Heya!

Thanks for giving *Kissed by Fire* a read. Did you enjoy Aria's adventure? Are you curious to see what's next in store for her and Declan?

I have good news and bad news.

The good news is that Burned by Fire, book three in the Blood & Magic series is available now! The bad news, Aria has a bumpy roller coaster ride in store for her and Declan.

Add in a gig with a Troll, and continued issues with the HAC and we have a recipe for disaster.

You'll love this next adventure. It's full of action and suspense with a twist around every corner.

Just follow the link and Grab your copy.

https://hi.switchy.io/BurnedByFire

xo Danielle

P.S. Reviews are like giving a hug to your favorite author. We love hugs. Please consider taking the time to leave a review for Cursed by Fire on Amazon!

P.S.S. Wanna chat? I love hearing from my readers, so if you're interested in staying connected, come visit me in my

Facebook group at https://www.facebook.com/groups/danielleannett

Binge the Complete Series

The Blood and Magic series is complete.
Meet Aria Naveed. She's a foul-mouthed, fire-wielding mercenary
who frequently manages to get herself into a pickle.

Thankfully she's good at getting herself out of trouble. *Most of the
time.*

See Burned by Fire on Amazon

Acknowledgments

Thank you so much to my **amazing readers** for bearing with me on this one. It took longer than I hoped to write, but I'm happy with the results and I hope you are too.

I'm still learning a bit as I go, and I appreciate your patience with me. This has been such an incredible journey.

Thank you to the **blogger community** for having my back. You guys rock! I never imaged the love and support I would receive and to say I am appreciative is an understatement.

Thank you again to **Jerica MacMillan** and **Deb**. You guys are amazing. You took my very rough story and helped me make it shine. Kissed by Fire would not be what it is without both of you.

About the Author

Danielle Annett is a Latinx Author. She's snarky AF, has three rad minions, and likes to write about kick butt heroines in volatile settings. Born and raised in sunny California she now resides in the Pacific Northwest, home to her Pacific Northwest Pack.

Sign up and get notified when Danielle has a new release: https://hi.switchy.io/AnnettNews

Find out more about Danielle here:
Website: www.Danielle-Annett.com
Amazon: https://hi.switchy.io/1AeV
Reader Group: http://www.facebook.com/groups/danielleannett
Facebook: http://www.facebook.com/AuthorDanielleAnnett
Bookbub: https://hi.switchy.io/AnnettBB
Instagram: https://www.instagram.com/authordanielleannett/
Goodreads: https://www.goodreads.com/author/show/7771866.Danielle_Annett
Audible: https://hi.switchy.io/ANNETTAUDIBLE

Stay in Touch

And before you go
Please consider leaving an honest review.
Reviews are like giving your favorite author a hug and we really love ***hugs!***

9 781953 264053